# CORPSE IN THE MEAD HALL

## A VIKING WITCH COZY MYSTERY

## CATE MARTIN

Cover design by Shezaad Sudar.

Ratatoskr Press logo by Aidan Vincent.

ISBN 978-1-951439-69-9

❀ Created with Vellum

# CHAPTER 1

*I* can't remember a time in my life where I didn't know I was an artist.

Not wanted to be. Knew I was. Even as a kid with a pack of crayons, I knew I was an artist.

But since moving to the North Shore to live with my grandmother and discovering I was a volva, which is sort of a Norse witch, but with lots of responsibilities beyond mere magic, I never seemed to have any time to just create art anymore.

Especially after I had started using my art skills to access my magic. I was still an artist, but, a few sketches here and there aside, all of my art was directed towards magical ends these days. It was almost never just art.

Mostly this was because between my ongoing education in all things magical and the number of murders I had found myself working to solve, I seldom had any downtime.

It was a recipe for burnout. I knew it.

But my chief teacher, Haraldr, seemed to know it too. Why else would he have arranged for me to have a day off? Well, really just a night off. One small lesson with him at lunchtime, sure, but after that, my evening was completely free. More than free. I had actual social plans.

Now, I was supposed to be using my time in the morning to catch a nap before meeting Haraldr at his house for lunch, but I was too keyed up to sleep.

Because that evening I was going to see my Runde friends again. After weeks... no, months. I was finally going to be able to sit with them and talk and laugh and catch up. It was only for a single night, but I didn't intend to waste a minute of it.

I really should have been napping to rest up, but after I had tried lying in my bed for nearly half an hour without being able to so much as close my eyes, I had given up. My grandmother had put me in a deep restorative sleep for more than a day, a sleep I had only just woken up from that morning, so it was hardly surprising that I felt, well, *restored*.

And so instead there I was, sitting in the comfiest chair in the living room of my house in the lost Norse village of Villmark, sketchbook resting on my knees as I looked out the window over the southern half of the village spread out on the hillside below me.

I had intended this to be a restful bit of sketching, a way to let my mind wander in something almost like a dream. I could hear the fire crackling in the fireplace behind me and smell the wood and ash faintly on the air.

Even louder than the fire was my polydactyl black cat Mjolner, purring away in his sleep on the pillow Nilda and Kara had given him as a housewarming present.

All perfectly pleasant. Even the coffee I had brewed when I had given up on sleeping was comforting. Most Villmarkers favored a highly caffeinated light roast that I found a bit of a challenge to drink on a daily basis.

Luckily, I had a friend who could move between worlds. Loke. He always brought back bags of French roast when Jessica got a new shipment from the supplier to her café. The rich, dark roast tasted so good I didn't have to add sugar or cream to get it down.

Plus, the amount of caffeine didn't make my hands shake as I sketched.

Alas, even with a steady hand, the subject I had chosen was a bit of a challenge. The landscape was lovely, rolling hills dotted with stands of trees. And the modernist architecture of the Villmarker houses favored just the sorts of lines I loved so much I could almost draw them with my eyes closed.

No, the problem was, being the middle of February in northern Minnesota, everything was covered in a blanket of snow. The sharp edges of the houses were softened under the bulk of the snow on their roofs, and the trees were similarly all but shapeless under their own wintery coats.

And there I was, with graphite pencil on white paper, trying to capture a scene that was really a bunch of shades of white and not much else.

It was a terrific drawing exercise, but not a particularly restful one.

I looked down at my sketchbook, then out the window, then down at my sketchbook again.

Nope. Definitely not right.

I tossed the sketchbook over my shoulder, intending to get another cup of coffee and maybe try again with a white charcoal pencil on gray-scale paper.

Only my sketchbook never hit the floor.

I turned in my chair to see Loke holding my sketchbook and examining my drawing. His brown eyes were so dark it was hard to tell what he was thinking, but he seemed to be transfixed.

"Don't look at that. It's a failed attempt," I said, reaching for the book. He took a step back, keeping the book away from my grasping hands.

"You're too critical," he said. "I think this is quite lovely. It's minimalist, in a way. And look, there's my house. Right there in that stand of lumpen shapes I know are my trees."

"It always draws my eye, ever since you pointed it out to me," I said. "How's your sister?"

"Esja is fine," he said, still studying my drawing.

"Coffee?" I asked.

He smelled the air. "Sure, that sounds good," he said. I suspected he shared my lack of enthusiasm for the usual Villmarker coffee. I took the sketchbook from him and put it in my art corner on the far side of the room. Then I headed for the kitchen, Loke strolling along behind me. "I have messages," he said.

"From?" I asked as I took another coffee mug out of my cupboard and filled it for him, then refilled my own mug.

"Everyone," he said. "Jessica, Michelle and Andrew will all be there tonight." He handed me several folded sheets of paper, then took a long sip from the coffee.

"Oh, good," I said, glancing at the contents of the notes. "I was worried they might be busy."

"Andrew had to switch shifts with some other guy, apparently, but it all worked out in the end," Loke said. "He's working as an EMT now, you know. Well, volunteering anyway."

"Yeah, he told me," I said. Loke raised an eyebrow at me, and I quickly added, "by letter, which you brought to me. I haven't been breaking any rules."

"Believe me, I know you haven't," he said. "More's the pity."

"You're going to be there tonight too, right?" I asked.

"If I'm able," he said.

"Why wouldn't you be able?" I asked.

"Oh, you know," he said with a shrug. I frowned at him.

"Is there something you're not telling me?" I asked him.

"Ingy, there's all sorts of things I don't tell you," he said. "Do you want to know what I had for breakfast?"

"Not particularly," I said. "Don't change the subject. You know exactly what I'm talking about."

"If you say so."

"There's a dark cloud hanging over you," I said.

"You see that with your magical vision, do you?" he said blandly.

"No, I see that because I look at you with the eyes of a friend," I said. "You know I will always be there to help you, no matter what's going on. You just have to ask."

"I know," he said.

"Is it Esja?" I asked. "You said she was fine, but-"

"How's Thorbjorn doing?" he asked, cutting me off. "Have you heard from him yet?"

The mere sound of his name gave my heart a pang. Just as Loke knew it would.

"How could I? I have no idea where he is," I said. "And it's only been a day. It's far too soon to be worried."

"Tell that to that little line that's furrowing your brow," Loke said, touching the same spot on his own face.

"I'm sure he's fine," I said. "But you're changing the subject again."

"Yeah, I'm good at that," he said with a grin. "There's nothing going on that you need to know about, Ingy, I swear it."

"Need to know, you mean as a volva?" I asked. "Because, like I already said, I'm talking to you as a friend. And I *want* to know."

"There's nothing *to* know," he said, setting his coffee mug aside. "The last few days have been exhausting, as I'm sure you'll agree. I brought you your messages, now I think I'll head home and check in with my sister if you don't mind."

I glanced at the time on my phone. "I should get moving myself. I'm having lunch at Haraldr's house, so I'm heading your way. Walk with me?"

"Of course," Loke said.

We went to the front door, and I pulled on my boots, then my parka, hat and gloves. The days were getting longer, but the weather was still unseasonably cold. I was so ready for spring.

But not so ready as Loke was, apparently.

"No coat?" I asked him. He was wearing his usual black tunic-length shirt on black pants, but his boots were meant for drier streets than what waited for us outside. He might be able to put his hands in his pockets - he usually did - but his ears were going to freeze without a hat.

"I'm comfortable," he said with another one of those careless shrugs.

But when he turned the handle to open the door, I pushed it closed again. It slammed shut with a bang as if the wind had taken it. Just as it always did. I had thought about getting it fixed, but decided I liked the fact that no one could sneak in without me knowing.

"How did you get in here, anyway?" I asked.

"It's not like you ever lock your doors," Loke said.

"No, but I never heard this door close. I *always* hear this door close."

"You were in the zone," he said, not quite making air quotes at me. "Seriously. I'm not your cat. I can't walk through walls."

"This is part of what you're not telling me, isn't it?" I asked. "When I first came to town, months and months ago, you said some things to me about your own sort of magic. You've never told me more about that."

"You picked your own path," he said with another shrug. "Speaking of which, Haraldr isn't the most patient of men. Since he's doing you this huge boon with letting you go to Runde tonight, you probably shouldn't risk being late for his lunch."

He smirked at me, but I knew he was right. I was going to be late, and I couldn't risk that.

"Fine," I said, opening the door again. "But at some point we're going to talk about this."

"Believe me, I have no doubt you're never going to let it go," Loke said.

We stepped out of my front gate and into the street, one of two that crossed at the heart of the village not far north from my house. It was late morning and the bulk of the shops were a short walk south of my house, so the street outside my gate was usually bustling with people.

Today was no exception, but this time, the usual shoppers with baskets over their arms or bags over their shoulders were hugging close to the garden walls on either side of the cobblestoned road.

I soon saw why: a small phalanx of warriors was marching uphill towards the center of town. They were dressed for the weather in heavy tunics and woolen cloaks, but I could also see bows and quivers on their backs and swords and axes hanging from their belts.

6

I recognized a few of them. Raggi and Báfurr for sure, but also some of their friends I knew only by sight and not by name. I had seen them before at Aldís' mead hall at the western edge of town.

But they weren't heading that way now.

"Where are they off to?" I asked Loke once they were safely out of earshot. Raggi and Báfurr were close to having a certain grudging respect for me, but it was a delicate thing still. And their friends liked me less. By blood I was only half Villmarker, and on top of that I hadn't grown up here. They were never going to let me forget that.

"Patrol, probably," Loke said and started walking down the road. I jogged to catch up with him. Cold as it was, I couldn't blame him for keeping up a vigorous pace.

"What do you mean, 'patrol'?" I asked.

"They're filling in for the Thors," Loke said.

"I thought Nilda, Kara and Valki were doing that," I said.

"Those three are guarding the ancestral fire and the caves behind the waterfall, sure," he said with a nod. "But someone needs to watch the village's other boundaries. For bears or trolls. The Thors are ranging quite far out, you know."

"I know," I said, and couldn't help sounding particularly miserable about that as another pang stabbed my heart. "You asked me before whether I'd heard from Thorbjorn. Is there some way I could?"

"You don't have a spell for that?" he asked. He sounded like he was joking, but I was pretty sure he was asking in all earnestness. With Loke, everything tended to sound like he might be joking.

"No. At least, not yet," I said.

"Pity," he said, but for just a split second I saw a hint of that old mischievous gleam in his eye.

"You take messages from me to my Runde friends," I said slowly.

"I do," he admitted. "But they all have doors. Thorbjorn is just out there, wandering." I had no idea what having doors had to do with it. And, maddeningly, he said no more.

I grabbed his sleeve and pulled him to a stop in the middle of the road. We were in the heart of the market district now, and several people had to quickly dodge around us, but I didn't care.

"Loke," I said warningly.

"Is there something you'd like to ask me?" he said, blinking innocently at me.

"You know there is," I said.

"Then say it, Ingrid Torfudottir."

"Can you get messages to Thorbjorn?" I asked.

"*You* could," he said, giving my shoulder a playful nudge.

"As I said, I don't know how," I said. "Do you?"

He sighed and was suddenly all seriousness again. "It's difficult. It has a cost. And a risk. But if the need is dire, I will do my best."

"So you can?" I said.

"Well, not for a love letter, I won't," he said. He was pretending to be offended. His moods shifted so quickly it was always a challenge to keep up. "You should run now before you're late."

"Yes," I said, glancing at my phone again. "But I'll see you tonight?"

"As best as I'm able," he said.

As cold as it was and as red as his ears were, he just stood there with his hands in his pockets, watching me as I jogged to get to Haraldr's house on time.

I looked back one last time before turning off the main road. He was still there, watching me. Then he waved a hand at me before turning and heading in the exact opposite direction than towards his house.

Where on Earth was he going?

Just the thought of that question made me shiver in a way that Loke in the freezing cold never had. Because it felt a little too on the nose.

Where in the entirety of the Earth, among all parts known to the modern world and hidden from it, was Loke going? And why?

One thing he had been right about. I wasn't going to rest until I knew.

But in the meantime, I had another rune to start mastering, and I really was going to be late.

I turned and sprinted the rest of the way to Haraldr's house.

# CHAPTER 2

*L*ike most of Villmark, Haraldr's house was built in a Scandinavian modernist design, all long sleek lines with lots of south-facing windows. The gray wood panels of its exterior made only the smallest of contrasts with the snow piled up against it, and I felt the urge to sketch again.

Definitely on gray-scale paper. If only I had brought my supplies with me.

Haraldr lived alone, and as I waited for my knock on his door to be answered, I realized I had no idea if he was a widower or if he had never married at all. The only member of the council I knew much about was Valki, and that was only because Valki was the father of the Thors.

The door swung open and Fulla, Haraldr's assistant, stepped back to let me in, her long blonde braids swinging with her motion.

"He's waiting for you in the breakfast room," she told me as she helped me out of my parka.

"Not the library?" I asked. "I was hoping we could get the lesson part out of the way first."

"I believe he intends to do both at once," Fulla said, hanging my parka on a hook by the door. I slipped out of my boots, then followed her on stocking feet down the long hallway that ran down the center of his house. His library was on the north side, where the books and other delicate materials he stored there would be kept out of direct sunlight.

His kitchen was on the south side, the blond oak of his cabinets shining brightly in the late morning sun. The breakfast room beyond it, with its floor to ceiling windows on two sides, was sunnier still.

"Ah, Ingrid," Haraldr said, and my dazzled eyes finally found him. Even with the light behind me, the midday sun caught the sparse hair that he had left glow like a silvery halo around his age-spotted scalp. He gestured with his wizened hands for me to sit across from him. The table was already spread out for lunch, with stacks of crispbread, thin slices of meat and cheese arranged on a cutting board, and a variety of fruits and vegetables on square plates all around the board. "I'm afraid I have a bit of council business this afternoon that I wasn't planning for. But rather than cancel our lesson, I was hoping we could cover it over lunch."

"Are you sure that's enough time?" I asked as I sat down across from him. "There are always so many meanings on top of meanings."

"Yes, but most of that I find you've been teasing out on your own through your meditations and art," Haraldr said. "Do you feel the same?"

"Maybe," I said, although in truth I wasn't at all sure I was ready to join the accelerated class.

"Help yourself," he said, waving his hands over the food. I started to build an open-faced sandwich on a slice of the crispbread, but before I was quite finished, he slid a square of paper across the table to me. I sucked a bit of spicy mustard off my thumb before picking it up.

The rune looked a bit like a triangular flag flying at half-mast. I had learned F and U already, so that meant this letter in the futhark must be Th.

"I think your cat knew what we would be discussing today," Haraldr said.

"My cat?" Then I saw him sitting in the chair between the two of us as if he, too, were about to have lunch. "Mjolner? When did you get here?"

Mjolner said nothing. Haraldr picked up a sliver of meat and set it on the table in front of the cat. Mjolner gobbled it up greedily.

"This rune isn't about cats, is it?" I said. I couldn't remember any of the runes being associated with a cat.

"No, it's about hammers," Haraldr said.

I looked down at the rune again. It didn't look like a hammer. The flag part might be the blade of an axe, but if it were a hammer, it was more the kind they made in the Stone Age than, well, Mjolner.

"Okay," I said, but the word drawled out of me, all unsure.

"It follows the other two," Haraldr said. "Can you tell me how?"

"The first was the beginning of all things in sort of an undifferentiated form. The second was molding that creation into a form. So this is more creation energy?" I guessed.

"What kind, do you think?" Haraldr asked, then bit into his own crispbread with toppings. A slice of cheese started to slide off the back end, but he caught it with a fingertip and pushed it back into place.

I looked over at Mjolner, who was watching intently for that cheese to fall.

"Explosive?" I guessed. "If this rune is related to Mjolner, that means it has a power like thunder and lightning, right?"

"And what would you do with such power?" Haraldr asked.

"Fight giants," I said, and felt my heart clench again. Just saying those words made me think of Thorbjorn. He had taken a nasty head wound in a fight against giants that I had accidentally caused.

Or I was just going to have to admit that lots of things were going to make me think of Thorbjorn, and there wasn't a thing I could do about it.

"Ingrid?" Haraldr said.

"Sorry. Distracted," I said. "So this is a rune of war and destruction, then?"

"The god Thor doesn't fight giants to destroy them, or at least that's not his primary purpose. He is only fighting to assert the rights

11

of humans to live their own lives, free from the interference of giants and trolls and those manner of creatures."

"So it's defensive," I said, picking up the card to look at the image again.

"To some extent," Haraldr said. "Is there anything about Mjolner you're forgetting?"

I looked over at my cat again, but his yellow-green eyes gave me no hints. It was almost like he was waiting to hear what I had to say.

"It's the opposite of destruction sometimes," I said, remembering a particular tale of Thor and the trickster god Loki where Thor had disguised himself as Freya and agreed to marry a certain giant who had stolen his hammer in order to get it back. "The hammer is put on a bride's lap during the wedding ceremony to bless the union."

"Indeed," Haraldr said as he assembled a second sandwich. "To bless a union with children. Like a lightning-struck tree. The lightning kills the tree, but it also allows something else to grow in its place."

I shivered. I had spent a night inside a lightning-struck tree quite recently. The Wild Hunt had been circling all around me. I wasn't likely to forget that night anytime soon. But that tree had kept me safe.

"So it brings forth life and protects it," I said. "That sounds like a good rune to use."

"Well," Haraldr said, but trailed off.

"Not always, I'm guessing," I said, and looked at the card again. "Lightning can be dangerous."

"Yes, but more than that, unpredictable," he said. "Chaotic, as the elements themselves so often are."

"I could accidentally summon a storm?" I guessed. Having been caught out on the waters of Lake Superior in the teeth of a magical gale once, I was in no hurry to repeat the experience.

"Storms serve no master," Haraldr said. "They would be a danger to friend and foe alike."

"Right. Duly warned," I said. I tried to turn my attention to my own food, but something was bothering me. "This rune is associated with chaos?" Haraldr nodded, but his eyes were eager, as if he knew I was on to something. "Giants are creatures of chaos, aren't they?"

"Are you surprised that the rune associated with Thor would also be associated with giants?" he asked.

"It doesn't seem fair to lump them in together," I said. "Thor is trying to do good, right?"

"Yes, but this isn't about ends. It's about means," Haraldr said.

My mouth went suddenly dry, and I was more nervous than ever at the idea of trying to use this particular rune. I took a sip of water, then looked at the card again. "There are lots of kinds of giants."

"Yes. You've already felt the presence of one kind, although you didn't physically encounter it."

"Fire giants," I said with a shiver. "This rune would potentially draw the attention of... what?"

"You can call them storm giants," Haraldr said. "Their usual name is like the rune. Thurses."

"Right," I said. I had heard that name before.

"I'm sure I don't need to tell you that you'll need to take extra care with dampening your magical glow while working with this rune. Particularly now, when our Thors are away."

"Maybe I should wait-" I started to say, but Haraldr reached across the table to clasp my hand almost too tightly in his.

"We do not have the luxury of time," he said. "We need you, and that need grows by the day. Just, be careful."

"I will," I promised. But then I found myself blurting out, "what's the council meeting about?"

Haraldr frowned at me. It was the darkest look he'd given me since the two of us had started working together.

"I'm sorry," I said, but then backtracked again. "It's just, if you need me to move so quickly from beginner to master volva, shouldn't you also need me to be aware of what's going on?"

"Not in this," he said. "Not everything that happens in Villmark concerns you."

"Okay," I said. But I felt more than a little hurt. What didn't concern me in Villmark? Trading issues or contract disputes or something similar?

But anything like that, he could just tell me. He could safely rely on the boring nature of the business to kill my interest.

"I know you're distracted by your plans for the evening," he said as he wiped his hands on his napkin. I was suddenly sure the council meeting was about my planned evening down in Runde. But then Haraldr gave me a sharp look as if he knew what I was thinking and was really hoping he didn't have to say again that not everything concerned me.

"I have my afternoon wide open," I said, picking up the card and putting it carefully into my pocket. "I'll get started on this right away."

"Don't push too hard," he said, the severe expression on his face finally softening. "I said you'd earned a day off and I meant it. Just see how it feels to you today. The real work can start tomorrow, when you will be less distracted."

"I can do that," I said, and we both got up from the table. I expected him to hurry away, but instead he walked me to the door and watched as I bundled up against the cold.

"Make the most of your time this evening," he said. I nodded, but my mind was running overtime trying to analyze his tone. Did he mean to make the most of it because it wouldn't be happening again for a long, long time?

No, surely he just meant to enjoy it because I had earned it.

He all but shoved me out the door before I had quite settled on which of those two scenarios I thought were true.

I looked down to see Mjolner sitting on the doormat next to me, ready to go home.

The minute we were back in our house, he returned to his nap on the pillow by the fire. I headed to my easel in the corner of the room and clamped a fresh pad of paper into place.

But I didn't start drawing right away. Instead, I closed my eyes and focused on my magical glow. My raw power shone bright and had a tendency to attract trouble of the magic-seeing and magic-wielding variety if I wasn't careful.

Luckily, I had gotten good at being careful. But this time, I made extra sure that none of my magic was shining out like a beacon. The last thing I needed was to attract an army of storm giants.

Only when I was positive that I was contained did I open my eyes and look at the blank page before me.

I started with my darkest, angriest, smudgiest charcoal. It felt appropriate for chaos.

I drew the rune over and over, rubbing the charcoal into the page with the edges of my hands until the shapes of the letters overlapped into dark gray storm clouds. I could feel the power of it, immensely strong but nearly impossible to control.

A little shiver ran up my spine when I realized what I had just thought to myself. Nearly impossible. Not *im*possible.

Thoughts like that were likely to get me into trouble.

I tore the top page away and began again.

By the time I stopped at sundown, there was a small mountain of discarded pages all around my feet. And my hands were black with charcoal past my wrists and halfway up to my elbows.

But I felt good. I felt like I'd just spent hours exploring this new shapeless power, figuring out how I and it fit together. I was getting good at this rune thing.

I went into my bathroom to scrub the charcoal from my hands, then looked at myself in the mirror. I only wanted to know if I had gotten any on my face. Of course I had, but that wasn't what caught my eye.

I leaned in to examine my reflection. Did I look different?

I felt like I looked different. But I couldn't point to any one change.

My hair was a tangled mass of red curls I should really make more of an effort to brush out whenever I put on and then took off my winter hat. It wasn't a good look, but it sadly also wasn't a new one for me.

My eyes were the same. I scrubbed the charcoal off my forehead with the corner of a washcloth, but the skin underneath was the same as ever.

Maybe I just felt different. I certainly felt more confident than I had the last time I had been in Runde. I was getting the hang of this magic thing. I wasn't remotely ready to take up my grandmother's mantle, but I was also far beyond what I had been capable of the last time I had seen my Runde friends.

Were they going to be able to tell?

Would they find it off-putting? Maybe even frightening?

I draped the washcloth over the side of my tub, then turned away from the mirror.

If I were being honest with myself, I wasn't really afraid that my friends would be terrified of me.

No, it would be bad enough if they just felt like I had outgrown them.

Not that I felt like I had. Not remotely.

But if they thought I felt that way, it would be just as bad as if I actually did feel that way. There would be a distance between us.

I really didn't want there to be a distance between us. I remembered all too well when my high school friends who had gone away to college had come back to visit. And there I had been, living in the same house, working the same job in the diner, taking art classes at the local college.

I knew how that distance felt from the other end of it. It was crushing. I had hated to be the one left behind.

I really didn't want to be the one leaving.

I gave myself a little shake, then headed to my bedroom to change into more festive clothing.

Because there was really only one thing I could do. I would just have to make sure that my Runde friends knew how much I loved and missed them. They were still a part of my life. Right now that was just through the letters that Loke was sneaking to me, but soon enough we'd be able to meet out in the open again, and not just for one evening.

Somehow, I had to let them know all that. And sadly for this, I couldn't really use magic. Or art. I would just have to be a really good friend.

I was pretty sure I could handle that. A normal night of mundane things was just what I needed.

But just in case anything abnormal happened, I tucked my new bronze wand up my sleeve before I left my house.

# CHAPTER 3

$\mathcal{T}$he sun was nearly out of sight behind the hills to the west behind me, and the stars had yet to emerge except for a few solitary pinpricks far off to the east. I knew they wouldn't light up the dark waters of Lake Superior much at all, but I couldn't resist the temptation to take a look.

I walked out to the very edge of the meadow that lay to the east of Villmark to catch the view.

The lake below was indeed nothing but dark gray water that stretched past the horizon on three sides of me. I could see the lights from a few fishing boats still out on the lake and further off the more orangish light from freighters chugging along the shipping lane.

I couldn't see the waterfall from where I stood, but I could hear it. The edges were frozen, but the central channel still poured over the edge, making the journey from Villmark to Runde faster than I was about to. I could see the river below, the ice giving it a silvery outline in the fading sunlight. The farms of Runde dotted all around it. And further east was the line of homes near the shore where the fishing families lived.

But the brightest object by far was my grandmother's mead hall. Not so much physically - in the colder months the torches that lined the outdoor spaces were never lit - but definitely magically. I could see the dense weaving of spells that protected that place. And even as I stood there looking down on it, I could see the glow from those spells pulse.

My grandmother was doing her nightly ritual to reinforce their magic. I should be down there, helping her.

I looked back over my shoulder, and the last sliver of the sun had definitely gone well below the hill line. No one could accuse me of going down too soon now. I found the small stand of stones that marked the top of the staircase down to the caves below and jogged down as quickly as I dared.

I followed the sandy-floored cave to the larger cavern, letting the light from the roaring bonfire within it guide me. Nilda and Kara were already there, standing close by the fire.

If someone were going to come to the North Shore to make a movie about valkyries, they would really have to cast the Mikkelsen sisters. When they were in armor with their complement of weapons, they looked like a Wagner opera come to life. Only think less heavyset prima donna and more mixed martial artist.

They weren't currently wearing their armor, and their weapons were stowed against the cave walls now that they were coming off of duty. But even in their leggings and roll-neck sweaters, they looked like Olympians having a relaxing evening by the fire in the Olympic Village between competitions.

I mean, I could clearly see the bulges of their biceps, and not only were they not flexing, they were wearing *sweaters*.

Kara was sitting on a stool and sharpening the point of a spear on a whetstone, but set it aside when she saw me.

But Nilda, on the other side of the bonfire, still hadn't noticed me. She was in deep conversation with Valki, who was halfway through taking off his cloak and wool coat.

"Hey," Kara said in a low voice, and I went over to her.

"Hi. What's up?" I asked, tipping my head towards the other two still talking.

Kara shrugged. "Valki is going to watch the fire while we're in

Runde with you. Although up until a second ago I was half convinced he wasn't going to make it."

"He just got here?" I asked. "From the council meeting? Haraldr left for that hours ago. What on Earth could they have been discussing all this time?"

"Council business," Kara said with another shrug. Then she called out to her sister. "Nilda? Shall we?"

"Yeah," Nilda said, but immediately turned back to Valki. "Thanks again for doing this."

"It seems pure frivolity to me," he said gruffly. But then he softened a bit. "But I suppose young people need a little frivolity now and again."

"Is there anything going on that I should know about?" I asked. "Any reason I should stay in Villmark?"

"No," he said. "Go. Haraldr promised you a night away. Just be sure to be back here before sunrise. No excuses."

"I will be," I promised.

Then Nilda, Kara and I followed the sharp turning at the far end of the cave to the larger space behind the waterfall itself. The air here was as damp as ever, and only a bit warmer than the air outside. I snuggled deeper into my parka, hands deep in my pockets, until we were out onto the rocky path. Then I needed both hands just to get down to Runde level safely.

"So, how was your first day without Thorbjorn?" Nilda asked teasingly.

"It's hardly strange for me to go a day without seeing Thorbjorn," I said. "In fact, that's more the norm."

Which was absolutely true. Even after moving to Villmark, I often went weeks at a time without seeing him. This time was no different.

Only this time *did* feel different. Perhaps because this was less a patrol of Villmark's boundaries and more of a scouting mission. But more because this time he had taken every one of his brothers with him. That had never happened before.

But I was sure the biggest reason I was missing him more this time was because people kept bringing him up and asking me to update them on my emotional state. That was definitely new. And not welcome at all.

"I'm a couple of weeks away from worrying about him," I lied.

"Yes, I suppose that's true. For you," Nilda said. I had no idea what she was talking about, but then I noticed Kara's cheeks were flushing a deep shade of rose and realized I wasn't the one actually being teased here.

Thorbjorn's younger brother Thorge had had a thing for Kara for years, apparently. But Kara had nursed a crush on Thorbjorn, and letting that crush go had been a bit of a heartbreak for her.

Now, I knew she and Thorge had been drawing closer to each other since Kara had nearly been abducted by the Wild Hunt, but I had no idea her feelings had gotten so deep, so fast.

But I could see they had.

We had left the steep, rocky slope of the path behind and were strolling alongside the river. She could no longer focus her attention on her hands and feet and had no excuse to avert her eyes when I looked at her.

Yep. She was in deep smit.

But also clearly very worried.

"I'm sure everything is going fine, wherever they are," I said. "If they had run into any trouble, Valki would know. And he wouldn't hide that from us."

"It's too soon to get concerned," Kara said.

"I said the same thing myself to Loke this morning," I said.

"Yes, she did," Loke agreed as he stepped out of the shadow of a tree that stood to the side of the path.

"There you are," I said. I had sort of assumed that he just wouldn't show up, but the happiness I felt at seeing him was tempered a bit.

He was still woefully underdressed.

"Doesn't the cold bother you?" Kara asked.

"Is it cold?" Loke asked, looking up into the deep indigo sky as if the answer were there.

"You know it is," Nilda said with a chiding click of her tongue. "Let's get him inside before he freezes to death out here."

"He can speak for himself, thank you very much," Loke said, but made no objections when each of the sisters seized one of his arms and propelled him across the snow-covered back patio to the door of the mead hall.

The door swung open and all the warmth and light from the massive fireplaces spilled out over us. The smell of burning wood and roasting meat and potatoes quickly followed it, as well as the sound of a multitude of voices laughing and singing and talking together.

Loke looked back over his shoulder at me and gave me a wink and a grin. Then he went inside the hall, one arm around each of the Mikkelsen sisters.

Had he shown up without a coat just to make that entrance?

I wouldn't put it past him.

Only there was clearly something else going on. It was like he was constantly finding himself locked out of his house when he'd intended only to quickly dash out for the mail or something.

Luckily, I was between murders at the moment. I had plenty of time to devote to the mystery of whatever was going on with Loke.

But after my night off, of course.

I stepped into the mead hall and pulled the heavy door shut behind me. I rose up on tiptoe to look around for any sign of my Runde friends. But as my eyes swept the room - taking in fishermen and farmers and craftsmen from Villmark and Runde alike, mixing without regard to the fact that half of them were dressed like modern day Vikings and the other half were dressed like 21$^{st}$ century northern Minnesotans - I could feel my nerves tightening up again.

They weren't there. Something had come up. Some EMT emergency, some problem at the café, some staffing issue at the restaurant.

Then I realized I didn't know where Loke, Nilda and Kara had gone off to either. I was standing there completely alone.

"Hey," someone said at my elbow. I knew that voice, although it didn't usually sound so tremulous and nervous.

I turned to see Andrew hovering beside me, as if torn between coming closer or running away. His dark blond hair had gotten longer and curlier since I had seen him last.

23

He also seemed shorter, but I knew that was dreadfully unfair of my brain to think. It was only because, after spending the last week or so in the company of Thorbjorn and a few of his brothers, everyone else seemed a little shorter. Really, it was nice to see someone I could look in the eye without craning my neck.

"Andrew!" I said and threw my arms around him.

He flinched. I could feel it. His whole body stiffened up and for a minute, I could sense him fighting the urge to step away from me, to put a little distance between us.

"I'm sorry," I said, letting him go and stepping back.

"No, I'm sorry," he said. "It's just... weird."

"It *is* weird," I agreed.

But he smelled the same. Of the damp wool from the fisherman's sweater he was wearing, which looked old enough to be a hand-me-down from his grandfather, if I didn't know for a fact that man was only half his grandson's size. But he smelled even more strongly of freshly cut wood.

I picked a shaving out of the knitted knot work on his shoulder, a little curl of some sort of whitish-gray wood. He glanced down to see what I was holding.

"I was working on something before I came here," he said.

"A boat?" I asked.

"No, something else," he said vaguely.

I opted not to press. The awkwardness between us was already at crushing levels.

"You guys coming or not?" Loke yelled from clear across the mead hall. I flushed half with annoyance and half with embarrassment, but then saw Michelle and Jessica waving at me frantically.

Michelle must have come straight from her job at the restaurant. She was dressed casually in jeans and a turtleneck, but her honey-blonde hair was still in its no-nonsense ponytail.

Jessica, on the other hand, looked like she had just come off the ski trail, in her thermal leggings and down vest and with her crown braid clearly showing signs of recently having been under a winter hat. Her cheeks were flushed with color, and although the interior of the mead hall was warm, I was sure that was the lingering effect of exercise in the cold February air.

"We should..." Andrew said, but indicated with his hands that I should go first.

Which was a good call, as I'm sure he was hoping to avoid the group hug that surely would've pulled him in had he been any closer.

Loke made no effort to avoid it.

Then we all sat down together at one of the circular tables further from the fire pit in the center of the room, and Jessica pressed a glass of mead into my hands.

"I want to hear everything," she said as she sat down beside me.

"About?" I asked.

"The Wild Hunt, just for starters," Michelle said from where she was sitting on the other side of me.

"What more is there to tell?" I asked. "I wrote you all letters."

"More details," Jessica said, pounding her fist on the table. Which was a very Viking thing for her to do, whether she knew it or not.

"I drew *pictures*," I said with a laugh. "Very detailed pictures. What more is there to say?"

"The tale must be told," Kara said.

"But first," Michelle said, picking up her beer and holding it aloft. "To friendship."

"To friendship," we all chorused, clinking our various glasses, steins and drinking horns (where had Loke found a drinking horn?) together.

Michelle and Jessica were grinning at me as we set our drinks back down, eager for the story I didn't even know how to tell. Even Andrew seemed keen to hear more, although some of the awkwardness was still there between us.

My mind was just starting to fixate on that, determined to figure out from his eyes and body language just what it was that he was thinking.

But then I just let it go. I was with my friends. We had an entire night to catch up. Not that I expected us to literally be up until dawn.

But surely somewhere in there I'd have a moment alone with Andrew, just a moment to talk.

In the meantime, I took another sip of my mead and sent a mental message to the god Odin, wherever he might be, to give my tongue the gift of storytelling.

And the gift of brevity. Because once my tale was through, I'd be passing the metaphorical baton on to one of them. And I wanted to hear everything.

The night couldn't possibly be long enough to hear it all. But we'd give it our best try.

# CHAPTER 4

Several hours later, we finally hit a lull in the conversation. I was still chuckling sporadically from Michelle's story about a misunderstanding between her and a pair of out-of-town customers at the restaurant. In fact, my whole body felt warm and bubbly from all the laughing we'd done together.

Jessica picked up her mug of beer to take a sip but found it empty. She frowned at the bottom of the glass, then looked over at the empty chair beside her.

"How long ago did Loke get up to get the next round?" she asked.

"Yeah, when was that?" Andrew asked, glancing at his phone. "It must've been an hour. Did he get hung up somewhere?"

I looked around the room, but there was no sign of him.

"I want another as well," Michelle said. "Let's go together, Jess. We'll see if we can find him on the way."

"Right," Jessica said and got to her feet. Then she pointed finger guns at Andrew and I. "You guys want another round?"

"No, I'm good," I said.

"I'm fine too," Andrew said.

"But maybe a bowl of something salty and crunchy?" I said. I had kept drawing so late before coming down to Runde that I had never eaten dinner, and lunch had been a long time ago.

"Sure thing," Michelle said, and the two of them made their way across the room to the tucked away corner where my grandmother served mead and snacks.

That left me alone with Andrew. I took a sip of my still mostly full glass of mead, even though I didn't really want it. I just wanted something to do, but that was too quickly done.

Andrew looked at his own empty mug, then pushed it away. He cleared his throat, and I leaned forward, expecting that he was going to say something. But he didn't.

"This is awkward, isn't it?" I said. "Why is it so awkward?"

"I really wanted to talk to you," he said earnestly. But he wasn't looking at me.

"We can talk," I said.

"No, not here," he said. "It's too crowded. Too noisy. Can we go for a walk?"

"Sure," I said, and slid my arms back into the parka I had left draped over the back of my chair.

We passed Jessica and Michelle waiting in line at the bar, but there was still no sign of Loke. I caught Michelle's eye and mimed that Andrew and I were stepping outside. She nodded and gave me a thumbs up.

The cold night air felt good on my warm face as we stepped outside. Then the door closed behind us and muted the sounds of voices from within.

We walked together across the parking lot and then down the road that led to the lake shore. Neither of us were speaking, but this time it didn't feel weird. It felt comfortable. How many times had we walked down this road together? It had been nearly every day when I had still been living in my grandmother's cabin.

Then we passed that cabin, and I looked at the back porch. The scene of our goodbye before I had gone to live in Villmark.

The moment when we'd so nearly kissed.

And just like that, the awkwardness was back. That kiss hadn't happened for a reason, and that reason was still there between us. He knew it as well as I. There was no point in discussing it.

We lived in two different worlds now.

"I miss Runde," I said suddenly. "I miss the view of the river from my grandmother's back garden. I miss my grandmother's breakfasts. I miss my little bed with its tiny window I can look out of with my head still on my pillow and see the lake through the trees."

"It's all still here, waiting for you whenever you come back," he said.

"I know," I sighed.

"But I suppose if you did come back, there would be things about Villmark you would miss," he said. His eyes darted over to meet mine for just a fraction of a second.

"That's true," I said. "I wish you could come up and see it sometime. I could give you the whole tour. There's a shop that specializes in wood carving that I would love to show you."

"Where that troll sculpture you bought came from?" he asked.

"Not that sculpture in particular, but lots like it," I said.

"I would like to see that," he said. "But I'm guessing that's still not possible."

"No," I said. "This night off is kind of a onetime thing."

"A reward for hard work?"

"Something like that."

"Then I'm sure there will be more," he said. "No one works harder than you."

"Well, I'm highly motivated," I said. "My grandmother needs help that I can't give her yet. Plus, what I'm learning is just so interesting it doesn't really feel like work."

He made a humming sound of agreement, but then we both fell silent again. The only sound was the road gravel grinding under our boots.

Was he ever going to get to whatever it was he felt he had to say? The reason we had gone outside in the first place? It was starting to feel like he wouldn't.

I supposed if he wanted to just let whatever it was go unsaid, I should respect that.

But I really wanted to know what he was thinking. And yet, I didn't want to grill him either.

I would just have to keep talking about myself until he volunteered something.

"I've learned so much since I moved to Villmark," I said. "But what little I've learned has just given me more perspective on how much I still have to learn. It's like I'm walking on a path that I thought led to the top of a hill, but now that I'm standing on that hill, I can see the path goes on. I can see this whole mountain ahead of me waiting for me to climb up it."

"I guess it's a good thing you find it interesting, what you're learning, then," Andrew said.

"I do," I said. "And Villmark is just the beginning. There are so many deeper worlds beyond it that I've just started to see."

"Loke has tried explaining it all to me before. I confess I can't quite wrap my head around it," he said.

"You talked to Loke about it?" I asked, surprised.

"Well, I'm curious," he said. "I try to imagine where you are, what it's like, what you might be doing. That hunting lodge you drew for me, for instance. That looked cool, like a piece of living history or something."

"It was," I said. "I should draw you more stuff, shouldn't I? Like what the town itself looks like, and the people that are in it."

"You should, but not just for me," he said. "You know, Jessica sold the last of your drawings in her café a couple of weeks ago. You should have Loke bring down more. I can make more frames for you."

"Right, I should," I agreed. I had totally forgotten that I sort of had another career, and apparently it was going pretty well. Not "hired to illustrate a children's book" well, but I couldn't achieve that goal without more effort on my part. I hadn't even tried submitting anything in weeks.

"What are you thinking?" he asked me.

"That you're right about the art," I said. "I don't quite have a rhythm to my days yet, so I don't know where I'll find the time, but I definitely shouldn't let my side hustle go."

"No, I meant in a larger sense," he said. I stopped walking and turned to face him.

"Is that what you wanted to talk about?"

"You never mention in your letters what you're thinking," he said.

"About?" I really wasn't following him at all.

He groaned in frustration, but I couldn't tell which of us he was getting frustrated with. I suspected it was himself.

"You're talking about my long-term plans?" I guessed.

"Sure," he said, but there was something dismissive in his tone. Like that hadn't been what he meant, but it was close enough.

"I mean, I was kind of talking about it when I was telling you about that mountain of knowledge I still have to climb," I said. "Was that not clear enough?"

"Not remotely, Ingrid," he said.

"I still intend to find a way to live as my grandmother does, both in Runde and in Villmark," I said. "But I'm a long way from getting to a place where I can do that."

"How far away?" he asked. "Months?"

"Years," I said.

His shoulders slumped down, like I had taken every bit of strength out of him with my words.

"Andrew," I said and reached out to touch his arm, but he stepped back away from me. "I'm sorry. All of this volva stuff just has to come first for me. I thought we were clear on this."

"Maybe we were," he said. "I guess I'm being silly."

I laughed at that. He looked up at me, almost shocked by my laughter. "Sorry," I said. "It's just, you and silly don't really fit together in my mind. Like, at all."

He grinned at that. "I can be silly," he said with mock defensiveness.

"No, I don't think so," I said. "Look, it was never my intention to make you wait around for me."

"I know," he said with a heavy sigh. "It's getting cold just standing here. Let's walk back."

"Okay," I said. My heart was aching for him. But I realized what I was really feeling was sympathy. Because I felt like I was waiting for Thorbjorn, and I had no idea when that wait would end. But there was no way I could tell Andrew that I knew how he felt because of *that*. Not unless I wanted to make it really awkward between us.

"You've been keeping busy," I said instead. "You wrote something about you being an EMT now?"

"Just a local volunteer, trying to get some experience," Andrew said. "I've been looking for paid work, but it's looking like I might have to go as far as Duluth to find a position."

"Oh," I said. Suddenly, this whole conversation made sense. "That's a bit too far to commute from here."

"Yeah," he said, sounding relieved that I understood. "The position I've been considering applying for would be four days a week, ten hours a day. That would give me three days a week I could be back here."

"That's not so bad," I said.

"I'm just thinking about it," he said with a shrug.

"Eventually something will open up closer to home?" I guessed.

"I hope so," he said. "It might take a few years. I'd need to build up my job experience first."

"Well, that sounds familiar," I said. "You and me, basically in the same boat."

"I hadn't thought of it that way," he said. "I guess that's true."

"And if you took that job, we wouldn't even be any less in touch than we are now," I said. "I'm pretty sure Loke could still get letters to you."

"Yeah, Loke can go anywhere," he agreed.

Just how extensive had Loke's conversations with Andrew about Villmark been? I had a sudden feeling that Andrew just might know more about Loke's particular brand of magic than Loke had ever shared with me.

But we were already back at the mead hall. From this angle, it

32

looked like any other run-down meeting hall, the parking lot full of old but reliable pickup trucks under the buzzing sodium lights.

Andrew grasped the door handle to let us inside, but I had a sudden bad feeling. Something was wrong. I wasn't looking at the building with my magical gaze, but I didn't need to. I could feel the spells in my bones.

And they felt wrong.

"Wait," I said, but it was too late. Andrew already had the door open.

And the scene inside was pure chaos.

# CHAPTER 5

*I*t says something that the body on the floor was not the most alarming thing.

In fact, it took me a moment to even notice it there. Partly that was because of the throngs of people crowding around it, blocking my vision.

But mostly it was because I was highly distracted by the sight of the spells, my grandmother's spells, failing all around the mead hall.

The ceiling was alternating between the dark smoke-stained wood rafters of the Viking-era mead hall and the water-stained, broken ceiling tiles of the Runde meeting hall. Even as I gaped up at it, I saw the edges of the effect washing down the walls, as if whatever was breaking the spell was a thick liquid running down like melted candle wax.

I wasn't sure if anyone else even noticed this yet, but they would soon enough. Because the other spells were unraveling as well. I felt a draft and knew that the spells that kept the interior warm and dry despite the structural inadequacies of both buildings were coming undone. I had no idea when exactly the mead hall in Villmark's space had been built, but it was definitely centuries ago. And the meeting hall that existed in Runde's space was several decades old itself.

I had no idea what would happen if the spells broke down completely. Two buildings definitely couldn't exist in the same place, but which would be dominant? Or would they just pull apart from each other?

That idea terrified me. Villmark and Runde were already so far apart. If that gap grew, how was I going to maintain a life on both sides of it?

All these thoughts rushed through me in a mere second or two, but it was a couple of seconds I didn't have to spare. But in my panicked state, I was going to have a very hard time shifting my focus to the magical world where I could see those spells and what was going wrong with them.

I pulled out my bronze wand and held it aloft, letting my eyes unfocus. At once, I could see the blinding light of the mead hall around me. I had helped my grandmother with her nightly ritual of shoring up these spells, so I knew what to look for.

I first felt relief wash over me when I saw no sign of anything attacking our place from without. Not that I wanted to think about what sort of creature could manage that.

But the sight of things just coming undone on their own was no comfort.

The spells that protected the mead hall were like knitted fabric. Sometimes they sort of snagged, and some loops were pulled too tight, others too loose, and sometimes they even started to unravel. What I had helped my grandmother with was like darning that pattern, pulling the gaps closed in a kitchener stitch. My grandmother could do this with such skill that those grafts never even showed when she was done. It was like the entire magic of the place became newly knitted fabric every night.

But that wasn't what I was seeing now. No, I could see gaps everywhere. They had been repaired, but sloppily.

And they were pulling apart all at once.

"Find my grandmother," I tried to say to Andrew, but he wasn't there beside me.

And that was when I really, properly noticed the body on the floor.

Andrew was kneeling beside the sprawled form of a man, desperately trying to revive him with CPR.

I told myself that whatever had happened had to have been from natural causes. A heart attack or stroke, even though the man had only the slightest sign of gray in his dark blond hair.

But the alternative was inconceivable. Or at least I would've thought so five minutes ago.

Because my grandmother wove spells throughout the mead hall that prevented acts of violence within its walls. The folk from Villmark and Runde mixed freely, and despite the excessive amounts of beer and mead that were downed on an average night, there was never so much as a fist fight.

But if even those most crucial of spells were pulling apart, that would mean the spells that made everyone from the modern world forget about Villmark were in danger too.

"Find my grandmother!" I shouted to whomever might hear me. Which was everyone; I flinched as I realized I had used my magically enhanced, commanding voice.

Everyone in the hall finally fell silent from their prior agitated furor that I had been tuning out. I heard footsteps running and hoped my grandmother would be with me soon to help.

But in the meantime, I had my wand. I set to work repairing the damage.

I had never done the nightly ritual alone, let alone this much more extensive spell work. I could see that my spells were not my grandmother's invisible kitchener stitches at all. They were darning up the holes and gaps in thick, heavy stitches.

But they were holding. I could feel a calm spreading across the hall around me as the panic that had only partly been about the body on the floor subsided.

I blinked back into the real world and instantly felt like the floor was sloping away from me. Then I lost sight of it in a wash of blackness that obscured my vision.

"Easy," Loke said as he caught me before I could fall to my knees. "Trust you to use an axe when a scalpel was all that was required."

"What?" I asked, more than a little disoriented.

"You should sit down," he said, and started to guide me towards a chair.

"No," I said, pushing myself away from him. "I'm all right. But someone needs to tell me what's going on here."

"He's not breathing," Michelle said from where she was hovering over Andrew, still performing CPR.

"Someone should call 911," Jessica said.

"No, wait," I said, but had to press my hand over my eyes as another bout of dizziness washed over me.

No one had called 911 yet? Either the spells unraveling had done more than make everyone really agitated, had affected their reasoning skills somehow, or less time had passed than I had thought.

Or maybe some of both.

"Ingrid?" Jessica said.

"I need to know what's going on first," I said. "This might not be a 911 problem."

"He's a human being," Jessica said earnestly. "Does it really matter if he's from Villmark or from Runde?"

"Andrew is doing everything he can," Michelle told her. "It doesn't look like it's going to be enough."

"Call," Andrew said as he switched from breathing to chest compressions. It was all he could do to get that one word out. I wasn't sure how long he could keep it up on his own.

"Loke, where's my grandmother?" I asked.

He shrugged, but before he could say anything, I saw Nilda and Kara coming up from the steps that were hidden behind the bar.

"She's in the cellar," Nilda said, her face pale and tight. "She's... not good."

I probably should've stayed where I was, in charge of things, making the crucial decisions about calling 911 and what else to do next.

But I didn't. The minute those words were out of Nilda's mouth, I was running, pushing past her and her sister to get down the steep wooden steps to the cellar below.

38

I had never been down there before. Luckily, I didn't have to go far. My grandmother was sitting on the broken concrete floor right at the bottom of the steps.

That was a jarring sight: my spry grandmother sitting on the ground, slumped half over like a discarded doll.

"Mormor," I said, grabbing her shoulders and giving her a little shake. She looked up at me, but very slowly, and even when she had lifted her face up to mine, it was like her eyes couldn't find me.

"Ingrid, let's bring her upstairs," Nilda said. "Kara and I can do it. We'll get her some tea or maybe something stronger."

"Mormor!" I said, leaning in closer to my grandmother's face. But she just blinked back at me.

"Ingrid, she's had some sort of shock. Just give her a minute," Nilda said. Then she gently pried my too-tight grasp off my grandmother's shoulders.

What had happened first? Had something shocked my grandmother and then the spells started failing, or the other way around?

I remembered all the sloppy patchwork in the spells. Whatever had happened here might have been sudden, but the groundwork for it had been in place for quite some time.

"Yes, get her some tea," I said, stepping back up the stairs. "Take care of her for me?"

"We will," Kara assured me as she and her sister lifted my grandmother gently up off the ground.

Getting her up those narrow steps between them was going to be tricky, but I didn't stay to watch.

I went back upstairs to deal with that body.

My wand was still in my hand, and as I approached Andrew and the victim, I started waving it before my eyes again. People from Villmark have a glow about them that was perceptibly different than people from Runde. Part of it was the ancestral fire that nurtured the entire community, bathing them all in magic.

But for people like those in the mead hall, who crossed the boundary between the worlds on a regular basis, the effect was even stronger.

39

There was no question about it. The man lying on the floor was from Villmark. But he was dressed like a citizen of Runde, in jeans, a flannel shirt, and modern work boots.

That was a bit unusual. Villmark had its own clothing industry, and while the usual clothing wasn't exactly classical Viking in style, neither was it entirely modern. The boots, in particular, were screaming to me that they were a clue.

But a clue of what, exactly? I still didn't know if this had been a heart attack or foul play.

"He was foaming at the mouth," Loke said to me as if reading my mind. "He was drinking by himself, back against that pillar, when he suddenly dropped his mug. That's when I noticed him. I heard the sound of it hitting the floor. And that foam around his mouth, it was like he was a rabid dog. Then he fell face-first down onto the floor."

"When did Andrew and I come in?" I asked.

"Right after," he said. "Boom, he's down, and people start crying out and getting excited, there's some pushing and shoving to either get closer to or away from that guy. And then you came in. Good work whatever you did to calm everyone down. For a minute there I thought there was going to be a riot."

"You know what that means," I said, and gave Loke a very pointed look.

"I do," he said. "It's not good."

"No, it's definitely not," I said.

Then Andrew sat back on his heels and wiped the sweat from his forehead. "Is there some sort of magic you can do to get his heart beating again?" he asked, gesturing towards the wand still in my hand.

"No," I said, putting my wand away.

"Are we calling 911?" Michelle asked.

"He's from Villmark," I said. "As much as he looks like he's from Runde, he's not. If we call the paramedics, they are going to have a lot of questions about him. Is there any hope at all that they can save him if we did call?"

Andrew wiped at his face again, but shook his head.

"Any chance this was a heart attack or stroke or something?" I asked.

"I'm not a doctor or anything, but I'd say no," Andrew said. "He had a lot of foam around his mouth."

"Rabies?" Jessica asked. It sounded like a joke, but the grave look on her face and the way she was hugging herself tightly said that it wasn't.

"Not likely," Andrew said. "If I had to guess, I'd say drug overdose. But is that even a thing in Villmark?"

"It's a thing everywhere, sadly," Loke said. "But not exactly common." Then he looked up at me. "Of course, drug overdose is just another way of saying poisoning."

Andrew frowned in a way that told me that when he was done thinking it over, he was going to agree. I seized Loke by the elbow and pulled him out of earshot of the others.

"You're saying murder?" I hissed at him.

"Don't you think?" he said.

"Murders don't happen here. They can't," I said, gesturing with one finger to the room around us. I wasn't sure if he could see the spells, but I knew he was aware of them on some level.

"But you and I both know that something just happened here," he said. "It would be nice to know what happened to our fellow Villmarker there on the floor, but that's just secondary, isn't it?"

I bit my lip, but I didn't need to answer out loud. We both knew he was right.

If the spells were coming down, this could be very, very bad for Villmark.

Unless I did something about it.

Only I didn't know where to start.

I looked back at the man on the floor, Andrew still kneeling beside him with Michelle's hands on his shoulders.

The spells going down and the man dying had happened at the same time. It couldn't be just a coincidence. I didn't know where to start with diagnosing the magical problem.

Luckily, I had a little more experience in investigating murders.

# CHAPTER 6

$\mathcal{I}$ sensed the crowd around me getting restless, and who could blame them? If we weren't going to move the body, they would prefer to leave themselves.

But I couldn't let them go just yet.

"I need just a moment of everyone's time, if you please," I said. I projected my voice to fill the hall, which it did nicely.

It also had the smallest undercurrent of magic to it. I wasn't commanding anyone to do anything, but I was nudging them a little, making each of them a little more open to hearing me out.

Then I turned to Loke, intending to ask him for advice on where to start.

Only he wasn't there.

He had been standing beside me just a second ago. Where could he have gone? He wasn't in the crowd around me, and I would've heard the sound of a door closing if he had left the building.

"Kara," I whispered to her, and she moved closer to me. "Where's Loke?"

"Wasn't he just here with you?" she asked with a frown.

"I thought so, but I guess not," I said. "Can you go stand by the door towards Villmark? I want everyone to stay here for me to ask just a few questions, or at least to know who is slipping away."

"So you don't need me to contain them here by force?" she asked.

I swear that bicep under her sweater popped.

"No, just ask them to stay. And if they refuse, tell me their name later. I'll have questions."

"Got it," she said, and swept through the murmuring crowd to the back door.

"The same on this end?" Andrew asked. He still looked beat from his efforts to revive the victim, but as always, he was eager to help.

"Yeah, you and Michelle at the front doors," I said. Michelle heard me and gave me a nod.

That left Nilda and Jessica to fuss over my grandmother. One of them had wrapped a wool shawl around her shoulders, a Villmark item of clothing that stood out jarringly against the red and black buffalo plaid of her flannel jacket.

She was holding a steaming mug of something in her hands, and I saw her take a tiny sip from it, but she still looked like she was out of it. Like she was only able to move on autopilot. Definitely not up for any of the many questions I had for her.

"First of all, does anyone here know who this man is?" I asked the room at large.

I looked from face to face, but everyone I looked to dropped their eyes and shook their heads.

"It's Dofri," someone said from the back of the room. Luckily the man who spoke was tall even for a Villmarker and I could see him over the heads of the others. I waved for him to come forward, which he did, if reluctantly.

"Did he come here with you?" I asked him. He was a lot younger than the man on the floor, closer to my age, but if they weren't friends, they still might be family.

But the man shook his head. "He lives near my parents. That's how I know him. But not for more than an occasional hello in the street."

"Okay," I said, disappointed. "Do you know who he *was* here with?"

He turned to look around the room. I could tell at once that he was skipping quickly over the faces of other Villmarkers. Then he pointed out two Runde residents who were standing close together near one of the pillars. A man and a woman. The woman took half a step closer to the man, but he took a matching step away from her, never even looking her way. "Those two."

"Thanks," I said, and crossed the room towards the two Runde residents.

The woman was a little older than I was, with hair a touch too aggressively bleached and skin that was already prematurely aging from sun damage. The man was a few years older, with brown hair still untouched by gray.

She was dressed for a night out at a much nicer club, with tight, dark jeans and a sparkly, low-cut top. Her bleached hair was teased away from her head, but it was also suffering from the dry, staticky winter air. It looked less like a hairdo and more like she was secretly touching one of those electric globes at a science museum. It seemed odd to me I hadn't noticed her before - she stood out a lot - but I had been pretty preoccupied and not exactly mixing with the crowd.

He, on the other hand, wore jeans that had been severely broken in. Not dressed for a date at all. No, he clearly worked in those jeans. And those boots, which were heavy duty, were clean enough but also worn with use. His flannel shirt and thermal vest were too common around Runde for me to have a clue if he was a farmer or a fisherman.

"Do you know who I am?" I asked as I approached them. The girl shook her head, then turned away as if dismissing me from her mind, but the man gave a cautious nod.

"You're Nora's granddaughter," he said. "I'm sorry, I don't know your name."

"Ingrid Torf.... Torfa," I said. I had almost said my Villmarker name of Torfudottir. That mouthful would raise questions for sure.

"Neil Nilssen," he said, and put out a hand for me to shake. It was warm, but roughly calloused. But again, he could be either a farmer or a fisherman.

"And you are?" I asked the woman.

She snorted as if put out that I didn't know her already. But then she said, "Mandy Carlsen. I've been out of town for a few years, but my parents still live down by the lake."

"All right," I said, and tried not to show that I didn't have a clue who her parents might be. I looked to Neil again. He seemed the more likely party to answer my questions. "You two were drinking with Dofri here tonight?"

"Not all three of us at once," Neil said, shooting Mandy a nervous look. Mandy ignored him. "He was here to meet me originally. But I wasn't with him when whatever happened *happened*."

"Did you see it happen?" I asked.

"No," he said, and tried to catch Mandy's eyes again. But she was looking past him, behind his back, towards the tall Villmarker who had pointed her out. She finally caught his eye and gave him a flirty wink.

Way to not let a friend's sudden death ruin a night out. I shook my head and turned my attention back to Neil.

"May I ask what he was meeting you about?" I asked Neil.

"Just a possible business venture, but it wasn't working out," he said. Then hastened to add, "but not in a bad way. We had just been feeling each other out, you know, but we'd both concluded that it wasn't going to work. No hard feelings whatsoever."

I didn't answer. I just watched his face. I could tell he was steeling himself to keep meeting my eyes. He was approaching "the lady doth protest too much" territory in my mind, but I didn't think he was outright lying to me.

"How long have you known Dofri?" I asked.

"Not long, and not well," he said. "We met here on a few occasions. Well, perhaps it would be more accurate to say we spoke together only four times. Tonight being the fourth. We weren't friends or anything. I don't know who his next of kin are or anything."

"So if I asked you if you knew any reason anyone would want him dead?" I asked leadingly.

"You think this was murder?" he asked, his eyes wide with

46

unfeigned surprise. "I wouldn't have a clue. Honestly. I barely knew the guy, but he seemed perfectly affable to me. Our interests didn't align in a business sense, but he was a decent guy. I have no idea who would want him dead."

He tried to shoot another look to Mandy, but she was still tuning us both out. She was scanning the crowd, like a girl at a bar who's with a guy that just bought her a drink but is still on the lookout for a better offer.

"Mandy?" I prompted, just fighting the temptation to get her attention back by snapping my fingers.

"What?" she asked.

"How did you know Dofri?" I asked.

"Who's Dofri?" she shot back. Neil made a little sound of protest. Whatever reason they had for standing so close to each other, he clearly had trouble tolerating her company.

"The dead man over there," I said. "You were here with him?"

"Not remotely," she said. "And I wasn't here with Neil either," she added.

"Okay," I said, not at all sure why she felt the need to spell that out. "Do you know what happened?"

"Heart attack? Who knows?" she said.

"It's a murder, and you might think about how glib you want to be in your answers," I said.

"I'll keep that in mind when the police arrive," she said with a scoff. Then she turned to walk away from me.

I narrowed my eyes, half in disgust, but more to focus on seeing the magical world.

But she was just normal Runde, as far as I could tell. She wasn't carrying anything magical, and she certainly wasn't magical herself. But I would have to sketch her to learn more.

If that would even work. It hadn't with Geiri. The powerful amulet he had been using to summon the Wild Hunt had been hidden from my perceptions by strong magic.

I hated not being able to trust my own instincts, and I hated feeling like I was in over my head.

But I really hated that this woman was just dismissing me. Even in Runde, I had earned more respect than that.

I was just reaching out to catch her arm and pull her back when the back door thudded open, slamming against the wall in a way that sounded like heavy wood against log walls and a steel doorknob against a matching rubber doorstop both at once.

Kara stumbled back out of the way, looking to me for directions. This wasn't the scenario we had discussed.

But it didn't matter what I would have said, not when all three members of the Villmarker council stepped into the hall.

Haraldr was leaning heavily on his staff, and I could see just how exhausted he was. He had been up since before the dawn and had spent most of the day in the council hall. Now here it was long past midnight, and he still far from sleep.

Valki behind him looked a little better. There were no weapons hanging from his belt, which was a relief to see. He wasn't coming expecting a fight.

Then I remembered that him being here left no one to guard the sacred fire. My stomach sank. This was huge, and not good.

He glanced at Kara, then stepped aside to let the final council member sweep into the hall. Brigida, she of the silver braids she wore like a crown around her head and the rings on every finger. I knew her the least of the three, and when she was the one to cross the room towards me, my stomach sank still further.

"Everyone is to leave this place at once," she said, waving one beringed hand over her head even as she continued walking towards me.

"They can't," I said. "There is a murder I have to investigate. I have only barely started questioning the witnesses."

"It isn't safe for anyone to stay," Brigida said. Her voice carried throughout the hall even better than mine did, and hers had no magical enhancement to it at all. Just good old-fashioned authority. I was a little jealous.

Everyone heard her words, and whether they were from Villmark or from Runde, they immediately started pushing towards the exits.

"Ingrid?" Andrew called from behind me.

"Please, this is important," I pleaded to Brigida.

"You know even better than I, I'm sure," she purred back to me, "that this place is not safe. Not now. Maybe never again. Get the people out of here at once. That isn't a request."

I turned to look at Andrew and Michelle, still trying to keep the Runde people inside the building. I gave them a hesitant nod, and they both stepped aside. The cold air outside rushed in, flickering the flames of the fires so fiercely they threatened to blow them out all together.

"Did Loke bring you?" I asked Brigida.

She looked surprised by that question. "That boy? I haven't seen him in weeks."

As unlikely as it had been that Loke would go fetch the council - he hated the council with all his being - at least it would've answered the question of where he had disappeared to.

And also the question of what had brought the council here.

"We do not wield magic ourselves," Haraldr said to my unspoken question. "But as you well know, that does not mean we have no awareness of magical happenings."

I thought he meant something about the spells protecting the mead hall, but before I could ask, Brigida was speaking again.

"This place is henceforth closed," she said to me. "If I have my way, it will never open again."

"I fixed the problem," I said, but perhaps the tips of my ears went pink or something. Something must have given me away, because I could tell by the arching of her silver eyebrows that she knew I was fudging that more than a little. "I did. I saw it was fixed. It's not pretty, what I did, but it works. And tomorrow, during the day when my grandmother is feeling better, we will do more extensive repairs. Everything will be tiptop by tomorrow night, I swear it."

"I'm sure you mean that," Brigida said. "But I think you're wrong. I think you're overestimating your own skill and Nora's power levels both."

I looked to my grandmother, who still sat with her shoulders slumped under that wool scarf. The mug in her hands had stopped steaming, but was still nearly full.

I turned back to Brigida. "She needs rest," I admitted.

"She does," Brigida agreed. "But more than you seem to think."

"Let's just see how things look in the morning," I said desperately, but she held up a hand to belay me saying more.

"There was a murder here, yes? That's why that man is lying flat on the floor?" she asked.

"Yes," I said, more softly than I would've liked.

"But that's not supposed to even be possible within these walls, correct?"

"Yes," I said, barely more than a whisper now. But then I forced my spine to straighten and my shoulders to pull back. I looked Brigida straight in the eye and said, "I'm investigating what happened."

"Of course you are," she said. "And I know I don't have to explain to you that your grandmother is your prime suspect. No one else could pull those spells down."

I just gaped at her for a long, awkward moment. Then I managed to say, "never in a million years will I believe my grandmother did this deliberately. Whatever happened, it wasn't that."

"Murderer, accomplice, *unwitting* accomplice," Brigida said, then danced her hand through the air dismissively. "I trust you will get to the bottom of it."

"I will," I vowed.

She nodded, but then she looked around the hall. Besides Valki and Haraldr, who waited by the doorway, all that remained of the night's patrons were Nilda and Kara, both standing by Nora, and Jessica, Andrew and Michelle close to the Runde doors.

And dead Dofri down on the floor.

"This building is closed," Brigida said to me. Then her eyes darted up and to the left as she searched her memory for one particular word. "Condemned," she said when she had it. "No one comes in. Lock the doors. Make it so."

She turned to leave, but I ran to stand in front of her again, barring her way.

"I have to investigate this. The victim is a Villmarker, but I have good reason to suspect the murderer is from Runde," I said.

She looked at me but said nothing.

"I have to be here to investigate," I said, pointing down to the ground under my feet. Then I realized that was really a place where Villmark and Runde both existed at once and swept my arms past her, towards Runde proper.

"We did tell her to be back by dawn," Haraldr said.

Brigida just barely avoided rolling her eyes. "Very well," she said. "Do as you must. Conduct yourself as you know you are expected to. If you do otherwise, we shall surely hear of it."

"Yes, I understand," I said.

And I was afraid that I did. I could be in Runde, but I had better be nothing but business while I was there.

The tricky part was that I would absolutely need my Runde friends to work on this investigation. I would have to be with them, talking together, and do it all without once seeming... well, friendly.

Brigida went out the door, Haraldr shuffling after. But Valki let the door swing closed behind them. He went over to my grandmother and made her meet his eyes. He whispered something to her, and she nodded, but still as if she was only vaguely aware of what was going on around her.

But she pushed the shawl back off her shoulders and set the mug aside. Then she raised her hands palms-up. She was moving so slowly, like she was underwater. But eventually she had them up over her bent head.

I felt a pull, like I was standing in the middle of a rushing river, all of it trying to sweep me towards my grandmother. I was blinded, and my ears roared with an indistinct sound like nothing I had ever heard before.

When it finally passed, I looked up to see my grandmother some-what recovered. She still looked tired, but more like a normal person after a long day. Not strange, since it was well after midnight.

But something was different in the magic around me. I wasn't normally aware of all the separate spells that enchanted this place acting on me, but I definitely felt them when they were gone.

And they felt gone.

I took out my wand and waved it before my eyes, then looked up, expecting to see that melting effect from when they had started failing before, but I didn't. There was nothing up there. Nothing at all.

The spells were all just... gone.

But if my grandmother had just pulled all of their power back into herself, there was no sign of it. There was no sign of magic in her at all.

"It's all right, Ingrid," she said to me. "It's going to be all right."

I didn't know what to say. I felt so suddenly bereft. I would blink and the hall around me would change from Villmark to Runde and back again. There was no overlap. There was just one place or the other, and I couldn't control which I saw.

Valki left my grandmother's side to walk up to me. His expression was as inscrutable as ever, but then he reached out a hand to clasp me warmly on the arm.

And that was the worst. That little gesture of sympathy from the last place I had expected to find it was making my throat swell with unshed tears.

Something was really wrong with my grandmother. There was only so long I could go before I'd have to face that fact.

"Nora should sleep in Villmark," he said to me. The low rumble of his voice was so like Thorbjorn's, it made my throat tighten further.

I nodded, then crossed the room to help her to her feet. I had no idea how I was going to get her up the rocky path. But then I realized that Valki was still there, waiting to help us.

I passed her off to him, then turned to my friends. "Nilda and Kara, one of you should get back to the fire. After what happened here, leaving that unattended is really not a good idea."

"I'll go," Kara said, and sprinted past Valki and my grandmother, out the back door and into the night.

"What about him?" Andrew asked. "We really should call the police."

"He's Villmarker. We'll have to bring him up to the village at some point, but for now, I think he just stays here," I said.

"Isn't there anything we can do?" Jessica asked.

"Actually, yes," I said, an idea just starting to form in my mind. "Can you guys wait on the back porch for me? I need to lock up, and then I'll need to run on ahead to make sure Valki leaves."

"We're going up to Villmark?" she asked. I could tell she was trying to contain her excitement under the circumstances. If she hadn't been, she'd be bouncing up and down like a kid whose parents just told her they were taking her to a theme park.

"Not quite," I said, and she deflated a little. "Just to the ancestral fire behind the waterfall. I want to try something, but I'm going to need your help. All of you, if that's possible," I said, looking over at Andrew.

"Absolutely," he said.

I watched the three of them cross to the back of the hall and go out the door to the patio. Then I looked out over the now-empty parking lot towards my grandmother's cabin.

This would be the first night she'd slept somewhere else in how many years? I was certain it was more like decades.

I closed and locked the front doors. Then I crossed the room to go behind my grandmother's bar. I avoided looking at Dofri lying on the floor.

But I did look up one last time to see if I could find any trace of the spells. They were definitely gone. I wasn't sure what the others saw, but for me, the place had finally settled in its Runde configuration. No amount of blinking was bringing the Norse mead hall back.

Until I knew what exactly had happened, I was afraid Brigida was right. The mead hall had to stay closed. It wasn't safe.

I found the key in the back of one of the drawers, a heavy iron thing that looked like it belonged on the ring of a guard down in a dungeon under a castle.

I went out to the patio and pulled the door shut behind me. Then I turned that key in the lock. It stuck, and I doubted it had been turned in years, but eventually it clicked shut.

The outside of the building looked like a mead hall, at least from the Villmark side of things. But the wood it was built from sat dark and mundane before my eyes.

It really was closed for business.

But only temporarily. I knew it was going to take a lot of work, but I wouldn't rest until I saw it open once more.

# CHAPTER 7

*J*essica, Michelle and Andrew were clustered together at the edge of the snow-covered patio. They had been up the path before, but never past the chamber behind the waterfall. And the one time they'd been there before, they had been guided up the path through a growing storm by Villmarkers. I wasn't surprised they were unsure of the way.

"Why don't you come up with me as far as the waterfall," I said. "I'll have you wait there while I make sure that Valki has gone into town."

They nodded and fell into step around me. The path ran for some ways beside the half-frozen river, but the moment the waterfall was in view I looked up towards it. I could just see a shadow moving around the last bend in the path. Valki and my grandmother were about to disappear behind the waterfall.

"Ingrid, what's the ancestral fire?" Jessica asked, and I looked away from the waterfall to pay attention to the path ahead of us.

"It was here first, before the village," I said. "Centuries ago, when my ancestor Torfa first brought her people here, the first shelter they had was in the caves behind the waterfall. Only later did they build the village, and still later did she craft the spells that hid it from others. But that fire from the first night has never stopped burning. Or so the legend says."

"Why are we going there?" Michelle asked.

"Mainly, I hope being near it will help bring my grandmother back around," I said. "It's a very powerful source of magic."

"You think that's what's wrong with her? That she's tapped out her magic?" Andrew asked.

"I don't know what's wrong with her," I admitted. "I don't even know what failed first, her or the mead hall. This is all so new to me, and no one in the village besides my grandmother can explain much to me about it. I just have to find my own way."

"She's been looking tired lately," Jessica said. "Whenever I ask her about it, she insists she's fine, but I don't know. This might not be a sudden change for her."

"I know. That's what I'm afraid of," I said.

"So I see why you're bringing Nora to the fire, but what about us?" Andrew asked.

But we had reached the steeper part of the path now, and the rocks underfoot were slick with patches of sheer black ice. "It'll be easier just to show you," I told him, and then we all focused on getting up the hill safely.

I left the three of them huddled together behind the waterfall, then pressed on towards the warm glow of the bonfire just around the bend in the cave.

I was worried that Valki would linger and fuss and be generally hard to get rid of, but when I reached the fire, I found that he had already left. My grandmother was sitting on one of the three-legged stools so close to that fire I was sure her knees must be burning hot. But she still had that exhausted look in her eyes and didn't so much as look up at Kara, who was bending over and speaking to her too low for me to hear.

"Valki said you should let her rest here for a bit before going the rest of the way," Nilda told me.

"That was my plan," I said. "I have a stash of art supplies somewhere around here..." I looked around, not remembering where I had stowed my spare art bag.

"It's in that chest there," Kara said, pointing. I lifted the lid and found not only the bag I had left there, but also a very modern collapsible easel and a ton more paper.

"Somebody's been adding to my stash," I said.

"If you had to guess...?" Nilda said leadingly.

"Thorbjorn," I said. "I told him my magic was stronger here, my drawings more detailed and helpful. But when did he do this?"

"I've never opened that chest before, so I can't tell you," Nilda said with a shrug.

"Are you going to invite the others in?" Kara asked. I looked up at her in surprise and she gave a dry laugh. "We're the guardians of the fire. We wouldn't be very good at our jobs if we didn't know when strangers, or in this case friends, were lingering on our doorstep."

"I wanted their help," I said.

Nilda nodded and went to lead them the rest of the way in while I set up the easel and drawing board, then pinned a fresh stack of paper to it.

"Is this going to be very involved?" Kara asked as she watched me sort through my pencils. Brand new, fresh out of the box. As stressful as this whole situation was, I still felt the same old excitement holding virgin drawing tools.

"I hope not," I said.

"Because I'm not sure the fire is helping Nora as much as a good night's rest would," she said.

"I know," I sighed, looking over at my grandmother still sitting as if half in a doze by the fire. "I know there are two people from Runde I want to talk to for sure. But I don't think they're likely to be suspects. I didn't get that sense about them. I just think they might know more than they thought they knew when I was talking to them before."

"How's that?" Kara asked.

"I didn't have the right sorts of questions to ask them," I said. "If I want them to confirm or deny things, or remember certain things they might've witnessed, I need to know the right questions."

"And drawing is going to help you?" But she didn't sound skeptical. Just interested in my process.

"I hope so. I want to get a sense of the room when everything went down. I want to see if there's anyone else I should be talking to, specifically someone from Villmark."

"This would be easier if the victim and murderer were both from here," she said. "Do you think you'll get that lucky?"

"Doubtful," I said.

Then Nilda came back into the chamber, Jessica, Michelle and Andrew close behind her. They were looking all around them with wide eyes, but there really wasn't much to see where we were. A fire, no different from any other bonfire. A collection of stools that were maybe a little old-fashioned, but not remarkably so.

The weapons against the walls were more interesting, but after their trip out on Lake Superior aboard an actual Viking ship, I suspected they had been hoping to see more.

"This won't take long. I know it's really late and you all have actual jobs to get to in the morning," I said. "Actually, Andrew, you didn't see anymore than I did, so if you have to go-"

"I'll stay," he said. He moved to stand behind me, leaning against the cave wall just out of my line of sight.

"Okay," I said, picking up a pencil and holding it poised over the paper. "I want to recreate the scene in the moments leading up to Dofri collapsing."

"I don't know how much help we'll be," Jessica said. "Michelle and I were talking to each other and not really paying attention to what was going on around us until it was too late. Sorry."

"No, I think you probably noticed more than you think you did," I said, already sketching in the lines that would define the architecture of the mead hall. That I could do from my own memory.

"He was standing at that pillar there when he fell," Kara said, pointing at a corner of my gradually emerging sketch. I wasn't surprised that he jumped in first.

"And before that, he was at a table back there, with that Neil fellow," Nilda said, also pointing.

Now all four of them were standing at my shoulders, watching the sketch gain definition. I could feel my hands already in the flow state, but my mind wasn't even part of it at all. It was only channeling things. I just listened and drew as the four of them remembered more and more details.

They were part of my art magic and didn't even consciously realize it. But as I had hoped, seeing the picture grow more detailed brought more and more additional details to mind.

"It was when we were still dancing, wasn't it, Kara?" Nilda said. "That's when he was at the table with Neil. Arguing."

"Pretty heated," Kara said. "Not loud enough to draw attention, though. They were close, sort of shout-whispering at each other."

"Then what?" I asked. The others watched the outlines of Dofri and Neil huddled together over the little table gained definition.

"Neil was about to leave," Jessica said suddenly. "I was still at the table, and Michelle was telling her story, but I happened to glance over and see him with his hands on the table like he was about to push himself up and away."

The outline of Neil's form changed, the old outlines still there but more ghost-like.

"But he didn't leave," Kara said. "He sat back down. The whole mood at that table just shifted."

"Okay, why?" I asked.

"That Mandy person showed up," Nilda said. "That upset Dofri."

"Upset, like anger?" I asked, my pencil bringing a form of Mandy to life beside that table. I might've overdone it with her crazy hair.

"No, but not happy to see her. More annoyed than angry," Nilda said.

"Yeah, Neil was sort of amused," Jessica said. "Like he wanted to stay now and see what Dofri would do about Mandy. Wow, I had no idea I was even paying attention to that."

"You certainly seemed to have been listening to me at the time," Michelle teased.

"Then what?" I asked.

They all stood silently for a long moment, and my pencil busied

59

itself with adding details to the room itself. The shadows cast by the fires, the carving in the roof beams and pillars.

I was tracing out a simple knot work pattern when Michelle suddenly said, "oh! I did see him! Dofri. He left that table, but he didn't go to that pillar in the front. At least, not right away. He went to the back of the room to talk to this really tall woman."

"Describe her," I said even as I sketched out another Dofri, this one at the back of the room.

"Tall," Michelle said again, but I could tell she was trying to summon more. "Blond just starting to go gray. One long braid down the back, like Nora wears hers. She was wearing dark brown leggings and a light brown top like a tunic on top of a turtleneck, I think. Clean and serviceable, definitely nothing fancy."

I kept drawing, but I could sense Nilda and Kara behind me leaning in as the face took shape.

It was a very detailed drawing of a face, far more detailed than anything Michelle had told me. And yet I knew it was correct. This was the woman who had spoken to Dofri.

"I don't recognize her," Nilda said and looked to her sister.

"No," Kara said, shaking her head. "I don't know her either. But a tall woman dressed like that, she'd have to be a Villmarker, wouldn't she?"

I didn't say it out loud, but I certainly hoped so. The alternative, some stranger from deeper in the hills, gave me chills just thinking about it.

Still, I'd recently met dwarves and moss wives I hadn't known existed a month ago. What more lurked so close to Runde but still hidden from me?

"Did they argue?" I asked. My pencil was beginning to slow, only adding a touch here and there over the crowded page.

"I don't think so?" Michelle said, clearly not sure. "I was telling my story at the time. I don't really know."

"I think they were still talking when we got up to go to the bar," Jessica said with a frown. "Dofri had a beer in his hand. He had taken it with him from the table and held it while he was talking with our mystery woman. Then he brought it to that pillar, far from anyone who was annoying him."

"It wasn't beer, it was mead. And it was still full," Michelle said, her voice full of wonder at her own recall of a very important detail. "He hadn't drunk from it yet. He had it at the table with Neil and Mandy and in his hand when he spoke to that woman, but he didn't drink it until he was alone. And he only took a sip."

"The puddle around him felt like a full mug's worth," Andrew said from behind me. "If this was poison, it was potent. And very fast-acting."

"I don't remember this woman," I said, touching the tip of my pencil to the woman at the back of the room. "I can picture all the other faces, but not hers."

"You drew her pretty well for not remembering her," Jessica said.

"No, that's not what I mean," I said. "I mean, I don't think she was in the room when I came back in from the walk up the road."

"You didn't tell us to keep everyone inside until a minute or so later," Andrew said. "She must've just gone out the back."

"Fleeing the scene of her crime?" Michelle guessed.

"Or just leaving because her conversation with Dofri was done," I said. "I'll have to find her and talk to her to know for sure."

"Now?" he asked.

"No, in the morning. I'm going to need help finding her, too," I said. As I spoke, my pencil was still wandering around the drawing, adding minuscule details.

"We can take turns at the fire. One of us could go with you," Kara offered.

"Thanks, I'll take you up on it if I have to. But it would be better if you two weren't distracted from the fire. I'll have to track down Loke," I said. Then I sighed, looking at the drawing. "Just where was Loke the entire time? He's not in this picture. But he was there when I came in. Does anyone remember?"

They all looked at each other, but there was nothing but shrugs and shaking of heads.

"Figures," I said, and pulled the drawing down off the easel.

"Thanks for the help, everyone, but I should really get my grandmother up to my house and put her to bed."

"I'll help you," Kara said, looking to her sister, who nodded her consent to be left alone.

"Ingrid, there's a limit to how long that body can just stay on the floor down there," Andrew reminded me.

"I know. I'll figure out what we're doing in the morning. Can I call or text you?"

"Anytime," he said, and gave my arm a squeeze.

Tired as I was, I couldn't help smiling back at him. All the awkwardness between us was finally gone. Being in investigation mode was just too familiar to us for that.

Even if this turned out to be a Villmarker affair, I knew I'd be going down to Runde at least once more to retrieve the body. It was nice to part ways with him and not have it be a long goodbye.

Someday soon, all of our farewells would be like that. But not yet.

In the meantime, I had work to do.

# CHAPTER 8

Kara helped me put my grandmother to bed in what had once been my grandmother's childhood bedroom. That felt weird, especially after we had tucked her in and I went down the hall to the larger room that had once been her parents'.

It just felt so wrong.

She had been asleep as soon as her head touched the pillow. I hoped it was a restorative sleep. I'd have to bug her later, when she was feeling better, to teach me that spell.

For my part, I got very little sleep at all. But it wasn't the events in the mead hall that were keeping me awake.

No, it was the constant, intense dreams of chaotic storms, dark twisting tornados, and walls of water washing over all of Runde that plagued me.

The last time I jolted awake with my heart pounding, I saw the sky to the east brightening, and even though dawn was still about an hour away, I gave up on trying to sleep. Coffee would be better.

I had a lot to get done that day, anyway. I might as well get an early start.

I got up and went to my closet to get dressed. Mjolner, curled up on his cushion by the bedroom fireplace, opened a single eye and glared at me accusingly. I guessed he had tried curling up on my pillow — his preferred place to sleep, pressed up against the back of my neck — but had been driven away by my restlessness.

I tiptoed past my grandmother's bedroom. Its only window faced north and didn't get enough morning light for me to see more than darker black shadows set against lighter gray shadows.

I shuffled more quickly down the stairs to the kitchen, so anxious for coffee that I could practically smell it.

I drew up short at the doorway. I hadn't summoned that smell of coffee out of my imagination. My grandmother had been putting it into the air when she had filled the basket of my coffee maker. The machine was just starting to gurgle to life as she stood with her back to me, putting the canister back in its place in my cabinet.

I felt an immense wave of relief. This was wonderfully normal. No matter how early I got up in the morning, my grandmother was always up before me. I was sure she was about to turn to my refrigerator and figure out what to make for breakfast out of what I had on hand.

Which wouldn't be much. I hadn't gone shopping yet since returning from my trip to the hunting lodge. I had only been gone for a few days, but I had thought it would be weeks when I left the house.

But it didn't matter since she didn't do any such thing. She just leaned back against the counter across from the coffee machine, arms crossed and eyes staring unseeingly at the floor as she waited for the coffee to brew.

My heart clenched yet again. She didn't look better rested at all.

I stepped silently back into the living room and found my bronze wand resting in its wooden box on my mantle. I brought it with me back to the doorway and waved it before my eyes as I looked at my grandmother.

She noticed this motion at once and looked up at me with a frown that quickly deepened into a scowl.

"I'm perfectly fine, Ingrid," she said, and there was a little bit of that old snap back in her eyes.

"Not perfectly, but better, I guess," I said, squinting at her through the blur of my waving wand. Then I tucked the wand away. "What happened to you last night?"

"I'm fine," she said again, more firmly this time.

"You're not answering my question," I said.

She sat down at the kitchen table with a heavy sigh. "Because I don't know the answer to your question."

"Well, can you start with why you were down in the cellar?" I asked as I sat down across from her.

"I just had to get a few more bottles of mead," she said. "Just like any other night."

"So you went downstairs just long enough to get a few bottles?" I asked. "You didn't have any by you when Nilda and Kara found you."

"No, I guess I didn't make it that far," she said.

"So the minute you stepped downstairs, Dofri died?"

She pressed a hand over her eyes. I thought she might be breaking down, but when she dropped it again, I realized she had just been trying to force a memory to the surface of her mind. "That must be how it timed out. But that's just a coincidence."

"When I came in, only seconds later, all the spells were unravelling."

"Yes, I felt that," she said. I would almost think she was being sarcastic if I had ever once heard her say anything remotely sarcastic before. I decided to chalk her tone up to lack of sleep.

"I didn't sense an attack," I said.

"No, neither did I," she said, more calmly now.

"You were in the cellar. I didn't quite get a sense of you either," I said.

"No, that would be true," she said. Then, before I could ask, she added, "the stone walls of the cellar are their own separate magic. The mead hall is infused with spells that predate me by generations, but the cellar's magic is all mine."

"Why?" I asked.

She gave me a sharp look. "Everyone needs a private space. And that goes double for a volva. There are many magics that work best when practiced alone. You'll learn that for yourself sooner or later."

"But you weren't practicing alone last night when the spells came apart?"

"I was just downstairs to get more mead," she said. "Ingrid, you're talking to me as if you think I'm a suspect."

"In the murder? Of course not," I said. She raised her eyebrows at me. "Mormor, I know you didn't kill anyone. I'm not even talking about the murder here. I'm just trying to understand what happened to all the spells. You heard what Brigida said, right?"

"Sort of," she said, looking down at her hands folded on the table in front of her. "Like out of a dream. She closed the mead hall."

"She ordered it closed, but actually closing it all down was you," I said. "You pulled every bit of magic out of the walls."

"I had to," she said.

"But I didn't see it inside of you after," I said. "Where did it go?"

"Just... down," she said, rubbing at her eyes tiredly. "Like a sprinkle of rain on parched ground. It doesn't matter anyway, since the mead hall is closed."

"Temporarily," I said as I got up to pour a cup of coffee for each of us. We took a few quiet sips. I could feel her bracing herself against me asking more questions about what happened to the magic. I decided to back up to the real matter at hand: what lead up to the murder. "I didn't sense any other power within the hall. Or outside of it, although I'm not sure if I would through that weave of spells."

"You would," my grandmother told me. "Especially if it were intending harm to the hall or those within it."

"So why did everything just come apart while you were in the cellar?" I asked.

"I honestly don't know," she said. "Nothing should have changed. Certainly not so quickly."

"But it wasn't quickly, was it?" I asked her. "Maybe the last blow was quick, but I when I was fixing the weave, I could see that the spell work wasn't right. The patches were-"

But she interrupted me. "I know what the patches were like. I did them myself. I know very well that they were rough."

"You needed my help," I said miserably. "And I was stuck up here."

"No, this isn't about you," she said, putting her hands over mine. "I've done this job for decades. I've been through times like this before, where it feels almost impossible to scrape together the energy to keep it all up."

"You have? What does it mean?"

"It just happens sometimes," she said. "These things wax and wane. Sometimes it takes a lot more effort to get half the work done, but you just do it. You put your head down and keep going until you get through to the other side and things just get better."

"You can't draw the power from someone else?" I asked.

She opened her mouth to answer, but then closed it again, a thoughtful look on her face. Then she said, "that's a tricky question. The short answer is no."

"Okay. And the long answer is yes?"

"It's more 'yes, but'," she said. "And it doesn't matter with the case at hand, which is where you focus should be."

I ignored her attempt to derail the conversation. "You've drawn from me. And when she was still here, you drew from my mother," I said, and she nodded. "Who did you draw from after my mother left but before I came to town?"

To my surprise, my grandmother laughed. "Well, I don't think he knew it, but from time to time I could pull a little power out of Loke."

"From Loke," I repeated. But it wasn't a question. It made too much sense. *Had* he known?

"Yes, but I wouldn't recommend you try that," she said. "His power is too unstable. Almost chaotic. Your control is years away from being fine enough to channel that."

I was nodding along with her assessment when I suddenly gasped. She gave me a questioning look. "He was there last night. Did he have anything to do with the spells unraveling? Did his chaos do it?"

"No, I don't think so," she said. "He wasn't in the hall when it happened."

"Yes, he was. He was there when I came in," I said.

"Was he?" she asked, frowning to herself. "No, when I went down the stairs, I know I wasn't sensing him. He had come to the hall with you and the others, but he had left again long before I went downstairs."

"But he was there-" I started to say.

"Think carefully," my grandmother told me and took a long sip of her coffee.

I closed my eyes. I remembered looking around the hall at all the spells. If he had been there, I would've noticed him. The people around me had been easy to tune out, their natural magic so dim compared to the glowing from the walls around us. But Loke? I'm sure he would've been brighter.

"He was there the minute I came out of my trance," I said as I opened my eyes. "He caught me when I started to fall. And it seemed like he knew what I had been doing."

"He infers a lot," my grandmother said. "And quite skillfully. You've been making leaps in your abilities since you've started studying with Haraldr."

"Mostly on account of the wand the ur-dwarves gave me," I admitted.

"Have you done any magic around Loke since growing so much stronger?" she asked.

I cast my mind back over the last few months. "I don't think so? You know, he disappears a lot."

"That he does," she agreed.

"But if he wasn't a part of what was destroying the spells, was it really a coincidence that he showed up the instant they were restored?"

"Oh, I doubt that very much. But I doubt even more that asking Loke will give us much of an answer. He doesn't so much *have* power as *is* power, and I don't think even he understands himself."

"Okay, let's table that," I said. Mostly because my head was starting to spin. "Is this related to the Wild Hunt? To the artifacts that keep turning up in town? To the Thors being away?" That last question in particular had me biting down on my lip in anxiety over what her answer might be.

"Any of that is possible," she said casually and finished off her coffee. She refilled it from the carafe, then asked with a gesture if I wanted more. But I shook my head. My cup was still three-quarters full. I took a sip, hoping that the caffeine would help me think.

"Why Dofri, though?" I asked.

"Yes, I've been asking myself the same question," she said. "I said that any of your theories were possible, but that's where they become doubtful. That's all pretty big magic. Too big to be used to eliminate someone like Dofri."

"You know him?" I asked.

"No. That's precisely my point," she said.

"The spells are supposed to prevent violence from happening within the hall. Does that include something like poisoning?" I asked.

"Of course," she said. "I serve food there. That may not be what my reputation is built on, but I'm still careful about the wellbeing of my customers. You can't even get a stomachache from undercooked potatoes under my roof."

"Normally," I said.

"Normally."

I took another drink of coffee. My brain was slowly starting to wake up, and I realized I was hungry.

Hungry, but with no real food in the house.

"How do the spells work? Do they just render the poison inert?" I asked.

She frowned into her cup. "You know, it's never come up. I believe I would just be aware of someone wishing another harm."

"So does it matter that you were downstairs at the time?" I asked.

"No, but that question doesn't even matter," she said. I raised my eyebrows at her. "Well, he wasn't poisoned when I was downstairs, was he? Not in the sense of the action taken by the murderer. The time I was in the cellar was just at the moment when he took the drink that killed him. No, whoever poisoned him, they put it in his drink much earlier. When I was still upstairs and should've been aware."

"The Freyas and Kara were lured outside by a potion that absorbed through their skin and was activated later," I said. "Something like that, would the mead hall spells read it as poison or magic?"

"In that case, it was both."

"Could this be both?" I asked. "Geiri knew how to hide magic from us. But he didn't figure that out on his own."

"Like I said, anything is possible," she said. "But again, why?"

"You're saying I need to figure out why Dofri was killed?" I asked with a sigh.

"The who and how would be helpful as well," she said. "Just let me have one last cup of coffee-"

But now it was my turn to interrupt. "No, you're not helping." She gave me an almost furious look, and I held up a hand to belay her objections. "Just for now! I have enough help to get started. Both here and in Runde. Let me do the preliminary stuff first. You need to focus on getting rest."

"I've slept enough," she said huffily.

"You and I both know that's not what I meant," I said. "If you don't recover, it won't matter if I catch whoever offed Dofri. Brigida and the rest of the council are not going to let you open the mead hall again."

"'Let,'" she scoffed.

"Mormor," I said.

"Fine," she said. "You go do what you need to get done."

"And you?" I asked.

She bit at her lip before answering. "I'll take a walk, I think."

"Where?" I asked.

She scowled at me. "Private places, young lady. I have places I can go to gather my energies. Don't you worry. If you need me, I'll be there."

"Well, that's always true," I said, and kissed her cheek before heading to my front door.

But before even pulling on my parka, I took out my phone.

The first item on my agenda? Finding out what Dofri had been poisoned with, if at all possible.

I touched Andrew's name on my contact list. He answered at once, as if he had left his thumb on his phone screen, just waiting to pick up my call.

"Ingrid," he said, sounding only half awake. I had to amend that first image. He had been sleeping with his phone in his hand, waiting to hear from me.

No pressure.

"Can you meet me at the meeting hall?" I asked.

"Yeah. Of course. What's up?" he asked, more alert now.

"It's time to call the authorities."

"I'll be there in ten."

I put my phone away and started getting layered up for the chill February morning. I had the beginnings of a plan for how to handle the police, but it all depended on Andrew.

Putting him in the middle of Villmark and Runde business was a big ask. I knew he would say yes. Without a second thought, he'd say yes.

I just hoped I wasn't about to put his fledgling career in jeopardy.

# CHAPTER 9

The morning air was cold and almost brutally dry. It was so dry it was nearly electric, like something in the air was building up and was about to explode. The loose strands of my hair not contained by my hat crackled with static as they clung to my cheeks, and the snow underfoot was like gritty bits of ice that shattered under my boots.

I was having flashbacks of my stormy nightmares from the night before. I almost expected to see the waters of Lake Superior rise up to engulf the whole shoreline.

The sky overhead was a clear, cloudless blue, and there wasn't even a hint of a breeze. Which would be more comforting if I knew I wasn't really fearing a more magical sort of storm.

I hurried through the caves, pausing only briefly to assure Nilda, who was sitting by the bonfire, that my grandmother was doing much better. Kara was sleeping on a cot nearby and we both kept our conversation brief and in whispers so as not to wake her.

Finally, I reached the back door to the mead hall. It was strange looking at it now. It still looked like the same building, but without any of the magical glow I was accustomed to. Once I had learned to see it, I had never again been able to tune it out.

But now the walls were just stacked graying logs, the roof sagging in places under the weight of the snow. It was like looking at the dead body of a loved one. What was loved about it was gone now.

Never to return?

I gave myself a shake and turned my mind away from such morbid thoughts. I let myself inside.

The interior was in its Runde meeting hall guise: scuffed linoleum flooring under water-damaged ceiling tiles, tables that all tilted one way or another and stackable metal chairs with cracked and faded plastic seats. I walked past my grandmother's bar, all of its warm wooden Nordic surfaces now chipped and cracked plastic-covered particle board, to the front doors. Then I pushed the bar to swing one of the doors open.

Andrew was there waiting for me, hands deep in his pockets and hopping from foot to keep his blood flowing. He darted inside. Although it wasn't exactly warm in that drafty old building, it was at least warmer than it was outdoors.

"One of those space heaters in the back must still work," I said, heading for the storage room that was behind the shelves of the very rudimentary general store my grandmother ran.

"It's okay. Let's just do this," Andrew said. Some hurt must've shown in my eyes when I turned to look at him, because he quickly added, "I'm sorry. That sounded awfully pushy. How is Nora doing?"

"Much better," I said. "She's taking the day for herself, going for a walk and just taking it easy."

"She's more than earned it," he said. "You know, someone in town can run this place during the day for her while she's recovering. I mean, everyone will be fine for a day or two, but long-term, this is the post office and everything. Runde needs it."

"You're right," I said, feeling terrible that I hadn't remembered any of that. "Even if the mead hall has to stay closed and Villmark can't extend down here anymore, it's too crucial to Runde for this place to stay closed."

"I can ask for volunteers. It's probably best if Nora picks who she wants to put in charge of the post and the store and that," he said.

CORPSE IN THE MEAD HALL

"But it's not going to be a night spot again anytime soon, I'm guessing."

"No, I don't think so," I said. "Even if we open the meeting hall in Runde in the evenings, it won't be the same. I mean, even now, no one in Runde really remembers why they love coming here because of the spells. But a night or two being in this place like it actually is?" I lifted my hands and gestured around the sadness that was the room around us. "I have a feeling people are going to decide to go somewhere else."

"It wouldn't be the same," he said. Then he looked around at the worn furniture and walls that had been touched by too many greasy hands since their last coat of paint. "It's already not the same."

"We're here to do what we can to bring it back," I said.

He nodded, then crossed the room to stand over Dofri's body. "You said you wanted to call the authorities. I guess that means that you know this wasn't magic?"

"It's complicated," I said. "My grandmother and I would've sensed most magic, but there are things that can be hidden from us."

"That's a horrid idea," he said.

"It's not common," I said. "And my grandmother is confident that wasn't the case here. I have people I want to talk to, and I plan to start with that as soon as we're done here. But I really want to know just what it was that killed Dofri so quickly."

"Magic wouldn't tell you that?" he asked.

"Not me," I said. "I don't know enough about poisons, or the sorts of plants that make poisons. And my grandmother is still recovering. I don't want to ask her to do anything that I can't find another way to do without her."

"So, we have a couple of problems," Andrew said, and I realized he had already been thinking over his end of things before he'd even stepped inside the meeting hall.

"Okay, tell me," I said.

"First of all, like you said before, he's not from this world. He doesn't exist in any computer systems or anything like that."

"Yeah, I thought about that," I said. "We don't have to even pretend to know who he is, do we? I mean, I know it's not exactly the tourist season, and this place is far from convenient from the highway. But still, so far as we know, he's just someone passing through town who collapsed here, in this place of business. We're as surprised as anyone that he has no ID and didn't leave a vehicle parked in the parking lot. It's weird, but weird things happen. There's no reason why that should bring suspicion down on any of us. Right?"

"I was thinking the same," he said. "But that leads us to the second problem. He's cold."

"Well, we just found him," I said.

"Inside the hall? At this hour?"

I glanced at my phone. It was nearly ten in the morning. "I came to open up and found him here like this. We don't know how he got in."

"I'm pretty sure I cracked his ribs last night attempting CPR."

"Who's to say you didn't do that now when we found him?"

"So it's 'we' found him now? Not you found him?"

"I guess so," I said. "You sure are grilling me hard on this."

"Yeah, imagine what it's going to be like when the police get here," he said. Then he looked up at me with a bit of a smile in his eyes. "You're a terrible liar."

"I don't know, I held up pretty well the last time the police grilled me," I said. Then I remembered. "The last time, when the spells were still functioning. When the police officer talking to me couldn't stop forgetting why he was here between questions." I sighed. "Well, what do you recommend?"

"I recommend that I call this in on my own," he said. "I'll tell just as much of the truth as I can."

"How's that?" I asked.

"Well, I'll say that I came here to open up because Nora is out of town. That's true. I'll say she was working last night, but she closed early because she was feeling under the weather. That way, if the time of death is accurate, it won't seem odd that no one here saw anything. He collapsed pretty close to normal closing hours, anyway."

"Normal for who?" I asked.

"Normal for businesses in the area that serve alcohol," he said with a dry grin. "I don't have to tell you your grandmother's been fudging those rules for years, do I?"

"I think the spells of protection linger over the patrons until they get home," I said. "That keeps them safe while driving home and by extension anyone they should find themselves sharing a road with. I'm telling you, my grandmother was very thorough. She takes the responsibility of protecting her people very seriously."

"Well, there's never been a problem, so maybe that's true," Andrew said. "So I came in, found this stranger on the floor, and tried to revive him with CPR until I realized he was too far gone. Then I called the police." He glanced at his own phone. "Which I should do soon if this story is going to work."

"He'll be a John Doe. They'd have no reason to tell us anything about what happened to him," I said.

"They might tell your grandmother since this is her place of business, but I don't think we'll have to rely on official channels in any event," he said. "I'm friendly with most of the officers that work this area, as well as the ER docs at the local hospital. And I'll certainly know the EMTs who take the call. One way or another, I'll know if they figure out the cause of death."

"And if they can't, it's probably magic," I said with a sigh. Then I said, "you know, if the murderer was also from Villmark, this could be an unusual poison. Like with Lisa last fall."

"I'll mention it," Andrew said, looking down at Dofri's body. "I was on the scene for that too, you remember? I spoke to the EMTs that night, too. I'll say this feels similar to me."

"Yeah, that's technically still an unsolved case, isn't it?" I said. "No one in Runde knows what we know."

"Things have definitely been different since you came to town," he said. "I should make that call."

"Give me just a minute first," I said, kneeling down beside Dofri. I reached out to touch his shirt, but my hands were shaking. I wasn't relishing the idea of searching a dead body.

"Let me help," Andrew said, dropping to his knees beside me. "What are you looking for?"

"I just want to be sure he doesn't have anything identifying on him. Or anything strange. Or anything magical," I said.

"I can handle the first two," he said, sliding his hands inside each of the pockets on Dofri's pants and shirt and vest. "What would something magical look like?"

"Probably jewelry," I said.

He checked all the pockets, then patted down the ankles in case Dofri had tucked something into a sock. Then he sat back on his heels, shaking his head. "Nothing."

"I didn't think so, but it was worth a look," I said. "Go ahead and call."

It was nearly twenty minutes before they arrived. Andrew had pushed for me to go and leave him to handle it on his own, but I had to be there. I wanted to see if the memory spells were still working.

The first officer on the scene was Foster, the very man from the county sheriff's office who had attempted to question me about Lisa's death months before. I waited inside while Andrew greeted him in the parking lot. Then the two of them came in together.

Foster pulled off his sunglasses and stood blinking in the doorway for a moment, waiting for his eyes to adjust after the sparkling whiteness of the winter morning outside.

Then his eyes passed right over me without the slightest recognition. "Is that the body over there?" he asked, pointing to where Dofri lay, now under one of the wool blankets from the back room of the general store.

"It is," Andrew said. "And this is Ingrid Torfa, Nora's granddaughter. I called her right after I called you."

"Ma'am," he said with a nod.

Yep, he totally didn't remember me. But was that old magic or new?

I stayed where I was sitting at one of the rickety tables out of the way as Foster took out his notebook and asked Andrew for the full story. Then he brought Andrew back around to the beginning of his story to clarify some details. Then he asked still more questions.

He didn't seem dissatisfied with any of Andrew's answers, which was good. Our cover story was holding up fine.

But he also wasn't remotely as confused as he had been the last time he had attempted to interview someone inside this building. He was, in fact, quite good at his job.

I looked up at the broken and stained ceiling tile over my head. There was not a single hint of magic within it or behind it. Those spells were definitely all gone now. It was going to be so much work, bringing this place back to life.

"Ingrid?" Andrew said, and I belatedly realized that he had said my name at least once before.

"Yes? Sorry," I said.

Foster looked at me with deep sympathy. "It's not unusual to be shaken up by this sort of thing, ma'am. Are you doing all right?"

"Yes, I'm fine," I said. "It's just, you're right. It's a bit of a shock."

"This place is a crime scene, I'm afraid. You won't be able to open today," Foster said.

"Oh. All right," I said, trying to sound like a normal citizen just told she was sitting in a crime scene. Like this was a new experience for me. I'm not sure I was very convincing.

"Ingrid, they're about to take the body to the coroners," Andrew said. "I'm going to ride along. Are you going to be all right from here?"

"Sure," I said. "Lots to do."

"I know," he said. "I'll call you when I hear anything. Is your phone going to work where you are?"

"Yeah," I said, and almost pointed out that it had worked that morning when I had called him, but bit that back just in time. "I mean, if I go for a walk, I might hit some dead spots. If I don't answer, text me."

"Typical Runde," Andrew said to Foster, who nodded politely.

"Here's my card if you should need to contact me," Foster said, handing me a generic sheriff's office card with his personal contact information written in pen on the back.

Poor Foster. He had transferred months ago. No one had ordered him his own cards yet?

79

"Thank you," I said, tucking the card away.

I had to leave through the front door. I watched as Foster stretched Police Line Do Not Cross tape across the door and then as all the vehicles left the parking lot one by one.

I stood there alone for a moment, listening to the sound of winter birds calling out to each other and the subdued song of the river nearby.

I had seen two corpses that morning. I hated to admit it to myself, but the corpse of the building was affecting me a lot more than that of the man.

But I had never even met Dofri. And the hall was so much more than just a place.

It was where two vibrant communities overlapped, where they met and bonded. My whole world didn't work without it.

I just had to get it back.

# CHAPTER 10

*I* wanted to talk to Neil Nilssen and Mandy Carlsen from the night before, but I didn't know where exactly they lived. I could probably find out pretty easily, though. I just needed to call Michelle. Her mother knew everyone in town and was handy with drawing maps to the more out of the way places.

But I didn't think they were suspects, and their usefulness as witnesses really would mean having very specific questions to ask them. No, what I needed first was a picture of who Dofri had been and what he had been up to.

Who I *really* wanted to talk to first was the mysterious Villmarker woman who had spoken to Dofri last. Neil and Mandy had given me at least some version of the events of the night before. But I had no idea what that woman had been speaking to Dofri about, or why she had left so quickly. And given she was from Villmark and hadn't approached their table at any point, I didn't expect talking to them about her would help.

What I really wanted to know was why she had left so suddenly. And had she left before or after Dofri had taken that sip, foamed at the mouth, and collapsed to the floor?

So, as much as I wanted to linger in Runde, the work really began in Villmark. I would have to take the sketch I had done and show it around. Someone must recognize the woman I had drawn.

I had left the sketch in my house, so after climbing back up to Villmark, I headed there first. I was just letting myself in my garden gate when the phone in my pocket buzzed. I pulled it out and saw a text from Andrew.

Just two words: no news.

I frowned as I tucked the phone back away and then nearly jumped out of my skin when I realized not only was I not alone; I had just been caught looking at my phone by the very last person I would want to know I had it with me in Villmark.

Brigida.

She was standing on my front step, a voluminous wool hood pulled up over the braided crown of her hair, putting her face in shadow. I had no idea what expression was in her eyes, but the down-turn of her mouth was distinctly displeased with me.

"I'm waiting for news about Dofri," I said, my words spilling over each other as they came out of my mouth way too quickly. "I'm hoping to discover what poison was used."

"Poison," she said, and her mouth twisted further.

"It seems the most likely cause of death," I said. "My grandmother and I have pretty much ruled out magic."

"Your grandmother," she said. This repeating my own words in the most sardonic of voices was getting old fast.

"Did you have something to say to me?" I asked, straining to keep my own tone polite.

"I did," she said. Then she stepped aside, clearly expecting me to open the door and let us both into my house. I took off my parka and hung it from a hook, but she kept her long, floor-dusting cloak on. She didn't even push back her hood.

She did, however, slip off her boots. Some things were too impolite, even for this woman trying to make a point. Tracking melting snow across any Villmarker's clean floorboards was high on that list.

I went into my living room and the two of us sat across from each other on either side of my cold fireplace. Mjolner appeared out of nowhere to hop up onto my lap, loudly demanding pets.

"I assume since you are awaiting news of the type of poison used, this means that Dofri's body is now lost to us," Brigida said. She was sitting stiffly in her chair, back ramrod straight and hands resting on the arms as if to deliberately display all of her many rings. Like she was sitting on a throne holding court.

In my house. On my chair.

"There might be a way to have his body turned over to us when the coroner is done with it," I said. Although I had no idea how I would manage to accomplish that, since the official story was that he was a stranger to all of us.

"Dofri had no close family," Brigida said. "If it is possible, it should be done, but the need is not dire."

"I also have a lead," I said, getting up from my chair to retrieve the sketch. I showed it to her. "This woman here is a Villmarker. Nilda and Kara didn't recognize her. Do you?"

Brigida took the paper from me and examined it closely. "I feel like I should," she said, but after a long pondering, she just handed the page back to me. "I'm sorry. I can't recall."

"That's all right," I said, folding the page so that it would fit into my pocket, but with the woman's face on top.

"Tell me, where is Nora?" Brigida asked.

"She went for a walk," I said.

"And where did she walk to?" Brigida asked, that bossy tone back in her voice.

"I don't know," I admitted. "She needed some time alone. She's overtaxed herself terribly, and she needs to recover."

"There's no question of that. It's been happening for months," Brigida said. I felt my cheeks burn, and she must've noticed because she added, "in truth, years. Your spending time here in Villmark, away from her, is not the problem. And she could always be here too if she chose. But she will never choose that, I fear. And that mead hall is such a needlessly extravagant drain on her power."

"I disagree," I said, and my face got even hotter as she pinned me with that imperious gaze. But I couldn't take it back now. "There needs to be a channel between this village and the rest of the world. If there isn't a safe one, then people will find dangerous ones. The mead hall is a safe space controlled by a volva. That's absolutely crucial to making this tiny village stay alive."

"Perhaps you are right," Brigida said. But then her voice grew stern again. "But that's no excuse for not keeping your grandmother in your custody."

"It's not like she's a suspect," I said.

Brigida pushed back her hood and fixed me again with her blue-gray eyes. "Actually, it's exactly like that. No one else had such an opportunity. She could control the spells. She has a knowledge of poisons second only to Halldis, who *is* in custody and always watched. She even serves drinks, including the very drink which killed Dofri the minute it touched his lips."

"This is crazy," I said. "She might have been capable of it physically, but never morally. But that doesn't even matter. She might have had means and opportunity, but she had no motive."

"Didn't she?" Brigida said, still staring me down with those eyes. Like she thought I already knew her answer, she was just waiting for me to say it out loud.

"I don't know what you're talking about," I said.

She sighed, drumming her fingers on the arms of the chair. "I'm not unaware of what passes in Runde," she said at last.

"Dofri is a Villmarker," I said.

"Yes, but he has ties to Runde," Brigida said. "Or rather, was looking to make ties."

"I don't understand," I said.

"How do I make it simpler?" Brigida asked herself. Then, to me, she said, "Dofri was a brewer of mead. He was looking to expand that from a past-time to a business."

"You think my grandmother killed him because she was afraid of the competition?" I asked. The idea was ridiculous.

"No, there's more to it. Dofri was looking to buy land in Runde. He felt that Runde offered something for bees that couldn't be replicated up here in Villmark. I can't imagine what that could be," she said.

"I know that honey tastes different when the bees get nectar from different types of plants," I said. "Beyond that, I have no idea. I would think anything that grew in Runde that lent itself to particularly good honey would also grow in Villmark."

"Then we agree on that score," Brigida said. "And yet, Dofri didn't want to replicate the honey in question up here. He wanted to just buy the land and the bees for himself."

"Hold on," I said, finally getting what she was driving at. "Are you saying Dofri wanted to buy Tuukka Jakanpoika's farm?"

"That is what I've heard," she said. "He supplies all the honey that your grandmother uses to make her own mead."

"He does, but I still don't believe that my grandmother would kill someone who was just outdoing her in a free market. Which wouldn't even happen, anyway. No amount of money in the world would persuade Tuukka Jakanpoika to leave my grandmother high and dry like that. And even if he did, and she never made mead again, she still has the hall. No one else can replicate that."

"If you insist," Brigida said. I could feel my temper bubbling up, but she held up a hand as if to forestall that. "All right, let's set the business interests aside. She still had a motive."

"What's that?" I asked, willing myself to stay calm.

"Tuukka himself, of course," Brigida said.

"What's that supposed to mean?" I asked.

"Surely I don't have to spell it out for you," she said.

"Could you do it, anyway?" I asked.

She heaved another epic sigh. "We on the council long assumed that her dual presence in our world and in Runde was because of your mother and you being out in that other world. She didn't want to risk losing contact with you, so she made sure there was a gateway between worlds."

"Okay," I said. That felt like the truth to me too, or at least part of it. I had no idea if my grandmother had started working in the mead hall before my mother had met and married my non-Villmarker father or if that had come after.

"But then why didn't she shut the place down when your mother died and you finally rejoined us?"

"Because she likes it?" I said, trying not to sound too sarcastic.

"Or she has another person in the larger world that is still holding her there."

"Tuukka?" I said. I knew they were friendly with each other, and I was pretty sure that Tuukka was nursing a crush on my grandmother.

But it never felt like my grandmother had reciprocated those feelings. Not even a little. They were friends who did business together. Nothing more.

"Okay, setting aside how that doesn't even make sense," I said, rubbing a hand over my face. "Tuukka wasn't even there that night. So what's this motive you're sure my grandmother has?"

"Dofri's offer was low," Brigida said. "Offensively low."

"Even if that were true, that would be between him and Tuukka, wouldn't it?" I asked.

"And your grandmother would never insert herself into the middle of such a situation to protect a friend?" Brigida asked.

I said nothing. We both knew she would totally do that.

"We don't know that she did," I said at last.

"Which is why I wanted to speak with your grandmother. She was seen recently confronting Dofri in the street outside his house. Her words were very heated; all the witnesses agree on that matter."

"When was this?" I asked.

"While you were away, hunting with your friends," she said with a dismissive wave.

As if I hadn't also been away because I was fighting the Wild Hunt. And sort of saving the whole town. Again.

"Did anyone hear an actual threat?" I asked.

"Not that I know of, but as I've said, I wanted to talk to her about it," she said. "But I understand Dofri was aghast at being so accused. He wasn't a man of many friends, but those who did know him say he was always a man of honor."

"If my grandmother were angry with him, she surely had a reason to be," I said.

"Perhaps," Brigida said. "Can you go fetch her for me?"

"What, now?" I asked.

"With your magic," she said. "I can wait."

"I'd prefer you didn't wait here," I said. "I have a lot to do, and no desire to disturb my grandmother. I know she didn't do this. And she needs time to recover. If she tells me that time has to be spent alone, I simply will not intrude on her. She's earned a little time to herself, and a measure of privacy."

"That's not acceptable," Brigida said.

"Well, you'll have to accept it," I said. But then I softened a little. "When I see her again, I'll send her to you. That's the most I'll promise. Well, that and to keep working on this case."

She stared me down for a long moment, but I refused to look away first. Finally, she shrugged and pushed up out of the chair.

"So be it. I expect to see her first thing when she's back in the village, and I will know if that's not true," she said.

"I'm sure you will," I said as I walked her to the door.

But she stopped just before stepping out to turn and face me one last time. "Oh, and that little device in your pocket? I expect to only hear tell of you consulting it for investigation purposes. I've been allowing Loke to bring you messages from your friends, but that is absolutely the limit. You swore an oath, and I expect you will uphold it."

I just barely stifled a grin, but the idea of Loke doing anything because the council allowed him to do so was pretty funny. I could just see the look on his face when I told him what she said.

But I managed to keep my own expression serious. "I have done and will continue to do so," I said to her.

I really wanted to give her a shove to get her out of my house, but I was on bad terms enough with the council.

But our little interview had changed my mind about one thing. As curious as I was about the mysterious woman that even Brigida didn't recognize, she wasn't where I needed to start.

No, if Dofri was looking to make a move into Runde, my investigation had to start there.

It was time to get directions to wherever Neil Nilssen and Mandy Carlsen were living. But especially Neil, who had also mentioned having a business relationship with Dofri.

I had a few specific questions for him now.

# CHAPTER 11

$\mathcal{I}$t was weird standing on the side of the highway again, not so very far from where my first investigation had started. I could even see the stump that was all that remained of the tree I had rammed my car into when I arrived in town. Nothing left but a jagged outline of black bark against the gray snow pocked with road salt and gravel.

I hadn't been down here in weeks, and as much as I'd love to sit in Jessica's café for a minute with a hot cup of coffee and a cinnamon roll, I couldn't spare the time.

Also, she looked really busy. Which was great for her, and kind of explained how all of my art had sold from where she had it displayed on her walls. She was getting tons of customers from off the highway.

As I approached the parking lot of the restaurant that Michelle ran with her mother, I saw it was packed full of cars with a couple more trolling through the lot, waiting for an opening.

It must be Sunday, a brunch rush. As an artist, days of the week had always been largely academic to me. As a volva, they were even more so. But I had waited enough tables to know that no one working inside would have the time to help me out, not even for as long as it would take to write down an address or draw me a map.

I mean, they would make the time if I asked. But there was no way I was going to put more stress on them. I'd been in their shoes too many times before.

So that plan was a bust. Luckily, up by the highway was the one reliable place to get a cell signal in Runde strong enough to use the internet. I pulled out my phone and did a little searching.

I took it alphabetically and tried to find Mandy first, but she quickly proved impossible to find using the massive results-generating power of the internet and not someone with local, specific knowledge.

I knew she was staying with her parents, and that her last name was Carlsen. The problem was there were several families named Carlsen in the Runde area. They were probably all related, and going to one would lead me to the correct family eventually, but I wasn't in the mood for that much door knocking.

So I switched to searching for Neil Nilssen. He was much easier. After just a few clicks, I had an address. Then I pulled up my map app to see if I could figure out how to get to where he was.

I recognized the area immediately. He lived right next door to Tuukka.

I started walking along the side of the highway, over the bridge that spanned the length of Runde down below. It was a hairy walk so close to all that truck traffic, but the alternative was to find a way across the river. There were no bridges down at town level, and even if it were frozen over, I would never trust ice over a river. My grandmother had a secret way to cross the river inside of Runde, but it wasn't one she had ever shared with me.

At least it hadn't snowed or rained recently, so the trucks that sped past me weren't also pelting me with anything thrown up off the road by their tires.

Still, it was a relief to reach the other side and take the first path down to the valley below.

While I was still reasonably close to the highway, I checked my phone one last time. No messages from Andrew, but it was still a little soon for him to have learned anything.

CORPSE IN THE MEAD HALL

I quick typed out a text to Loke to see if he was free and able to run down leads with me. By the time my bars dropped from one to zero I still hadn't heard back from him, but that was far from unusual for Loke. I put my phone away.

Tuukka's farm was tucked close against the bluffs that circled Runde. He was the closest person on this side to the boundary of Vill-mark, although so far as I knew, he was no more aware of its existence than most of the rest of Runde.

I had been to his farm a few times as a child, memories I had only recently recovered. Since getting those memories back, I had been mainly focusing on remembering my time in Villmark, especially my adventures with Thorbjorn. But now that I was seeing familiar land-marks around the footpath, I started to remember my time here as well.

I could almost taste the fresh honey dripping from the comb. I even remembered going out to the hives once with Tuukka, all geared up in an over-sized beekeeper's outfit complete with netted hat. I had watched as Tuukka smoked the hives, then lifted the lids to let me look inside.

How could I have forgotten that? It had been so thrilling at the time; I had half-convinced myself to give up my artistic dreams and pursue beekeeping as a career.

The thought was troubling, but not because of my childhood dreams.

No, it bothered me because it reminded me of what Frór had said about my grandmother's spell to block my memory. How she had overdone it. I had assumed at the time he meant she had used too much magic because she had been so very angry at the time. But what if that wasn't it? What if even back then when I was a child her powers were already getting erratic?

I wished I had asked more questions before Frór had gone away. But it was too late now. He was even farther away than Thorbjorn and his brothers were.

My thoughts were so consuming that I caught myself halfway up

91

Tuukka's front walk before I remembered that his house wasn't my destination. Then I had to backtrack to the last house I had passed.

It was a nice-looking place, not extravagant by any means, but very lovingly maintained. A cozy little farmhouse complete with smoke rising up from the chimney.

I took out my wand and waved it before my eyes. There was no hint of magic, not that I had thought there would be. But I did get a brief glimpse of what lay hidden there by the drifts of snow, a picture of this farm as it would look at the height of summer.

There was a line of trees between the two properties, but on Neil's land, apple trees that extended from the road clear down to the river. The vision of them was so vivid I could almost taste the golden apples sweet and tart on my tongue.

Almost out of sight behind his house, I could see a large pumpkin patch. Neil could supply all of Runde with jack-o'-lanterns from that patch. I saw a few larger gourds closer to his back door, probably intended for the county fair or even the state fair competitions.

The back of his property was all brambles, but those brambles were blackberry and raspberry bushes. I could see the berries peaking out in bursts of pink and purple. Clearly, my picture-perfect agricultural vision was spanning a few growth seasons, but that just felt right to me. I was seeing everything at its best as I looked at it.

And over all of it, I saw a cloud of bees happily pollinating every blossom they could find. Their buzzing filled the air like a happy hum as they worked.

It was indeed a perfect little farm, but it was bursting at the seams. I doubted a team of agricultural scientists could find a more efficient way to maximize the output per acre.

I put my wand away and knocked on the door. I heard the shuffling of feet within and then Neil himself stood in the open doorway, cup of coffee in hand.

"Ingrid Torfa," he said. "Why am I not surprised to see you?"

"Our conversation last night was interrupted," I said. I wasn't sure how much he even remembered of the night before, given how erratic the spells had been, but he nodded.

"Come on in," he said. He waited as I pulled off my boots, then led the way through a living room that felt completely unlived-in to a kitchen that was far more homey. "Would you like some coffee?" he asked.

"Sure," I said, taking a seat at the table near a window that over-looked Tuukka's yard. I could just see the tops of the hay bales that I knew Tuukka had put around his hives in the fall to protect his bees from the cold winter winds.

I was distracted from that view by Neil snatching up a coffee cup that had been on the table in front of me when I sat down. He put it into his sink, then fetched a fresh one from the cupboard. He filled it with coffee and handed it to me before pouring the remains of the coffeepot into his own cup. Then he sat down across from me with a heavy sigh.

"Do you live here alone?" I asked conversationally.

"I do since my mother died," he said.

"Oh, I'm sorry," I said.

He waved that off. "It was four years ago."

"It looks like you're doing quite well," I said. "Do you get a lot of families coming by for apple and berry picking? Pumpkin stands by the highway?"

"I do all right," he said, but I could tell that my question surprised him. I supposed not many people could tell all that by looking at his farm in February.

"It must be handy being so close to Tuukka's bees," I said.

"Oh, you know Tuukka?" he asked.

"Of course. He's close with my grandmother. She only uses his honey in her mead," I said.

"Right. I'd forgotten," he said. Which I didn't think was actually true, but I decided not to call him out on it. Yet.

"Tuukka is getting on in years," I said instead.

"He's young for his age," Neil said. "We help each other out with two-man chores and he's not much less capable than I am at anything."

"Still, there may come a time when you will need bees of your own," I said.

He frowned at me and set his coffee cup down on the table with a little click. "Your grandmother sent you."

"Sent me to do what?" I asked.

"You know what," he said, and got up to bring his cup to the sink, turning his back to me as he did so.

"I know that Dofri was inquiring about buying Tuukka's farm," I admitted. "But that seems strange to me. I don't think Dofri is in a position to handle the... financing."

"I made Tuukka an offer months ago. A very reasonable offer," he said. He ran a little water into his sink and added a squirt of dish soap. I had to wait for the water to stop before I could speak again.

"He turned you down," I said. I got up from the table to lean against the counter beside him, watching him as he washed first one coffee cup and then the other, setting them in the empty drainer beside the sink. The entire kitchen spoke of a very tidy bachelor. The floor was a bit grungy if one looked very closely, but the counters were immaculate.

"He has no children. No heirs. The offer I made to him was to buy his land, yes, but not to move him off of it. I well remember how my father was in his last years. He farmed until the very end, with no question of ever stopping. I know exactly how Tuukka would feel about anyone trying to make him stop, too," Neil said. He rinsed the last of the soap bubbles down the drain, then dried his hands on a towel.

"What was the offer?" I asked.

"Full market value for his property. He could continue to work it for as long as he was able, and all the proceeds from his honey would still be his. I just wanted to learn the trade from him while he was still able to pass his skills on. And, of course, the house would remain his for the rest of his days," Neil said.

"That *is* a very generous offer," I said.

"Tuukka has always been a good neighbor. I've known him my entire life. Why would I want to try to rip him off?" he asked.

"But he still turned you down," I said.

"I don't know why. He never told me," Neil said. He turned to lean against the counter beside me, arms crossed as he glared down at the floor.

"I'm just confused. I understand my grandmother was angry because what Tuukka had been offered was a bad deal," I said.

"That wasn't me," he said.

"Was it Dofri?"

He made a noncommittal sound. Well, I doubted he had heard about my grandmother yelling at Dofri in the middle of Villmark. But he surely knew more about Dofri's offer than most.

"All right, tell me one thing. Was Dofri working with you or against you? Were you competitors? Was Tuukka planning to sell to Dofri for some reason, and that's why he turned down your offer?"

"Like I said, I don't know why he said no to me. But I didn't exactly press. A no is a no. I moved on," he said.

"But this *is* why you were speaking with Dofri last night, right?" I prodded.

That question seemed to irritate him a lot more than it should. He almost growled before pushing away from the counter. "I think it's time for you to go. I've lost enough time in dealing with you people. It may be a Sunday in the middle of February, but I still have chores you're making me late for. If you please." He made a sweeping gesture for me to follow him back to the front door.

But I didn't move. I just frowned at him. "You people?"

"It's been nothing but questions, and I've had enough," he said angrily. "I had nothing to do with what happened to Dofri. And I don't have to discuss anything with you people, even if I did. If it truly was a murder, that's a police matter. Not... local gossip."

There it was again. You people. Plural.

"So it wasn't the police that were talking to you first?" I asked.

"No, it wasn't," he bit back. "Please, I really must ask you to leave."

"Who was here, Neil?" I asked.

"I never caught his name," he said.

"But you let him in your house?" I asked.

That seemed to give him pause. He stared off into the distance beyond the kitchen window for a moment. "I kind of knew him, or at least I recognized him. He's a regular down at your grandmother's lodge."

"What does he look like?" I asked.

Now he scowled at me. He reached for my elbow, but I took the hint and headed towards the front door without letting him touch me.

But as I put my boots back on, I pressed again.

"What did he look like?"

"Tall," he said, the shortest of all possible answers.

"Hair, eyes?"

"He was wearing a hat with a brim. I saw neither his hair nor his eyes to speak of," he said.

"What kind of hat?" I asked desperately.

"He was wearing work boots, jeans, flannel shirt, a parka and a trucker cap. Happy?"

Not remotely. That description fit nearly every single male in Runde.

"I'll probably be back for more questions," I said as I stepped outside.

"Don't bother. From this point on, if you don't have a badge to show me, I'm not saying another word."

Then he shut the door with a slam.

That could have gone better. Not only had I not learned anything new, I hadn't even confirmed anything Brigida had told me.

But as I walked away from his house, what was on my mind wasn't the questions I hadn't gotten answers to. It was just who it was that had been there first to talk to Neil.

The coffee cup on the table when I sat down had still been half full and gently steaming. Whoever it had been, I had missed them by just minutes.

Had they known I was coming? Had they seen me go by when I had kept walking on autopilot towards Tuukka's house?

And why had they fled?

Had I just missed catching the murderer? Or had I inadvertently thwarted a second attack intended to take Neil out?

I wanted to sit down in the snow in Neil's front yard and draw it all out, see what my magic could uncover.

But I had left my art bag back at my house in Villmark.

I made a mental note to ask my grandmother what her shortcut was. Then I headed back up to the highway, taking the one way I knew back home.

# CHAPTER 12

$\mathcal{T}$he minute I had finished climbing the steep path back up the level of the highway, my phone rang. I stepped back from the noise of the road as far as I could, then took the call.

"Hey," Andrew said.

"Hey," I said back. "What did you learn?"

"Not much. You sound out of breath?"

"I was just at Neil Nilssen's farm, next door to Tuukka. I'm about to cross the bridge back towards home," I said. I turned my back to the highway to look out over the lake, always a better view.

"Do you think he's a suspect?"

"My gut says no," I said. "But he's involved somehow. What did the medical examiner say?"

"They've eliminated most basic poisons. But since I mentioned Lisa, they're doing a more thorough check now. Most of that involves sending samples to an outside lab."

"How long will that take?"

"Sending the samples? Already done. Getting the results back? Sometimes weeks."

"Yikes," I said.

"I have to go back to the meeting hall and let a tech in," he said.

"You have a key, right?"

"I do, actually," he said.

I could tell he was holding back something. Something he didn't want to tell me, and he was stalling.

"Andrew?" I said leadingly.

"They want to test your grandmother's mead," he said. "All of it. That means opening every single bottle. It's going to ruin any batches she's currently fermenting."

"She's not going to like that," I said.

"I tried to pretend I didn't know what Dofri was drinking, but someone had figured it out from the spill on the floor," he said.

"And?" I prompted.

He sighed. "Apparently, Nora never had the correct licensing to make and sell her own alcohol. They're threatening to shut down the whole lodge."

"Great," I said.

"When the mead comes up negative for any contaminants or poisons or whatever else they're looking for, I'll work on getting her legal to open again," he said.

"Andrew, that sounds like an awful lot of work," I said.

"It probably is, and I'm sure it's going to be a huge bureaucratic headache. But we need that place open, don't we?"

I didn't answer right away. I wasn't sure what he meant by 'we.' The people of Runde? Of Runde and Villmark together?

Or just he and I?

"I should probably let you go," he said.

"Wait," I said. "Have any police started questioning witnesses yet? Or is there a P.I. working the case or something?"

"No to the police. But a P.I.? In Runde?"

"Not too likely, right?" I said.

"Well, it's just, who would've called them? Dofri isn't even from Runde."

"Yeah, I guess," I said.

"Why do you ask?"

"When I was talking to Neil just now, he had already been questioned by someone else. A tall man in a work clothes and a trucker cap, so dressed like anyone else around Runde."

"That doesn't sound like a P.I. to me," Andrew said.

"Neil said he didn't know the man or what his name was. Of course, he could've been lying about that. But he said he knew him from the mead hall. Or I guess he called it the lodge."

"I can double-check if anyone else might be on the case."

"That would be great," I said. I pulled the phone away from my ear to glance at my screen, but I had no text messages. "Say, one last thing. Have you heard from Loke at all?"

"No, but that's not weird."

"It's not long enough to be weird on my end either, but I wish he'd get back to me," I said.

"If I talk to him, I'll pass on that message."

"Great. Thanks."

There was a long pause, as if neither of us wanted to be the first one to hangup. But then a truck blasted past me, lying on their horn at a car that had just made a risky pass in a no passing zone before reaching the bridge. By the time that noise had faded away, Andrew had disconnected.

Nearly half an hour later, I opened the door to my house in Vill-mark to get hit full blast by the aroma of meat cakes in rich tomato sauce. Apparently, my grandmother was both home and stress cook-ing. My stomach growled loudly, impatient for me to get my parka and boots off and head for the kitchen.

My grandmother was just piling plates in the sink when I came in. Plates, plural.

"What's going on?" I asked. "I thought you'd be out all day."

"That had been the plan this morning," she said as she dried her hands on a towel. "There are meat cakes left if you're hungry."

"Starved," I said. She slid a couple of cakes from the cast-iron skillet onto one of my plates, added a generous dollop of mashed potatoes, then spooned the last of the sauce over all of it. The beef was seasoned with nutmeg and cloves and cooked in butter, and there was just a hint of cream in the potatoes.

This was why home-cooked lunches always made me want to take afternoon naps.

My grandmother turned back to my sink filled with soapy water. I ate and watched as she washed two glasses and two plates with forks and spoons to match, stacking them one by one in my drainer.

"Who was here?" I asked at last.

"Oh, Roarr," she said absently.

"Roarr?"

"Yes. I actually came across him on my walk, and he wanted to speak with me, so I brought him back here and made him lunch."

"I had no idea Roarr merited such treatment. These meat cakes are fantastic," I said, not at all embarrassed to be speaking with my mouth full.

"Thank you, dear," she said.

"What did Roarr want to talk to you about, if I may ask?"

"Oh, this and that," she said. She filled the kettle with water, then set it on the stove to boil. "Tea?"

"No, thanks. I wasn't intending to stay. I just came home to get my art bag, but then I smelled all this."

"I'll probably head back out myself," she said. She fussed over choosing a tea bag and putting it in a mug.

"Mormor," I said. "Why was Roarr here? Was it about what happened last night?"

"Not really," she said. "I don't believe he was even there. He didn't mention Dofri at all. He was just talking to me about Tuukka."

"About the bids on his land?" I asked. "I spoke to Neil Nilssen about that this morning. I know he and Dofri both were trying to buy Tuukka out."

"No, not about the land," she said. "It was about the honey."

"Tuukka's honey?"

"Yes. Roarr was just curious who else besides me bought honey from Tuukka," she said.

"And?" I prompted.

"Well, I told him what I'm telling you. I don't rightly know," she said. "You'd both have to ask Tuukka."

I made a mental note to do just that. Then I asked, "why would Roarr care who Tuukka sells honey to?"

"I didn't ask," she said, nudging the kettle to sit a little more directly over the heat.

"He was here long enough for you to make lunch, and this wasn't a quick whip-up of sandwiches," I said.

She turned away from the stove to look at me. "Most of what we discussed was personal. Roarr is still dealing with things. From time to time, he comes to me to talk things over. None of it is relevant to your current investigation. If it were, I promise I would tell you."

"Right," I said, a little ashamed for grilling my own grandmother.

"It's possible he's considering what line of work he wants to go into," she said as she turned back to the stove. "There are a few other brewers of mead in town. To the best of my knowledge, they all buy their honey from beekeepers up here in Villmark. But perhaps Roarr is thinking about trying his hand at it."

What a coincidence. First Dofri and now Roarr.

If only I believed in coincidences.

"Did he ask anything about how it's done?" I asked.

"No, but he did ask if anyone had offered to buy out my business," she said. She glanced back over her shoulder at me. "The answer to that is another no."

"Did he make an offer of his own?" I asked.

"Not to me," she said. The kettle whistled, and she shut off the flame on the stove, then poured the boiling water into her waiting tea mug.

"If he were talking to you because he wanted to start brewing his own mead, he seems to have avoided most of the relevant questions," I said. "I don't like it. I think he's up to something."

"I would think if that were true, I would've sensed it when he was speaking to me," she said almost testily.

I wasn't so sure that was true anymore. But instead I said, "maybe he's asking you questions on someone else's behalf."

"Like who?" she asked.

"I don't know. Brigida, maybe," I said. Then I mustered up my courage to say, "she thinks you should be considered a suspect, you know. In fact, she wanted me to tell you to go see her the next time I saw you. It's up to you whether I actually saw you just now or not."

"Don't be silly. Half the town saw you come inside, and they knew I was already here," she said. "But thank you for your loyalty, dear."

"So, how is Roarr doing?" I asked.

She was blowing on her tea to cool it, but set her mug back down to consider my question. "Better than I've seen him in a long time, actually."

"Did you sense anything going on with him?" I asked, waving my hands around as if that somehow conveyed "using magic."

"Not how you mean it," she said. "No, I think he's just coming out of his current stage of grief. If he is looking at finding work to occupy his time, that's a very good sign. And he seemed interested in things in the world in a more positive way than I've seen him since Lisa died."

"If?" I asked.

"Oh, you caught me," she said with a gleam in her eye. She took a sip of tea before going on. "The only other reason I can think of for Roarr to be asking me about honey and mead businesses would be that he's looking for another place to spend his evenings. He prefers mead to beer, you know."

I gave her a puzzled frown. "What do you mean 'another place to spend his evenings'?"

"Well, my mead hall is tangled up in his memories of Lisa. He's never comfortable there anymore."

As far as I had seen, Roarr wasn't comfortable anywhere. But I kept that thought to myself.

"And since everything with Bera, he's not really comfortable in Ullr's hall either."

"That's a shame," I said, and meant it. I had forgotten how caught up with Bera and her crimes he had been. "Maybe I *should* talk to him. If Loke and the Mikkelsens were all there, maybe he'd be able to enjoy it better."

"My mead hall or Ullr's?" my grandmother asked.

"I was thinking Ullr's," I admitted. "Mormor, you know there's a chance we won't be able to open the mead hall again."

"The council will come around," she said with a dismissive wave of her hand. "You and I together will be able to recast those spells even stronger than they were before. Don't think I haven't noticed how much more power and control you have than even a few weeks ago."

My cheeks heated at the rare compliment from my grandmother.

Then she said, "if more power than control, I notice."

I couldn't argue with that, so I didn't even try. But there was more I had to tell her. "There's also a problem in Runde. You know you never had any sort of license to sell your own mead to the public, don't you?"

"As far as anyone in the larger world knows, I'm not selling anything at all," she said blithely.

"Well, they kind of know now," I said. "They are testing your mead in case something in it was the cause of Dofri's death."

She scowled, a far darker look than I was used to seeing on my grandmother's face. "I should be down there now, then. I will have this turned back around soon enough."

"No, don't go," I said, catching her arm before she could get up from the table. "It's too late to stop them from testing the bottles, or to stop the rest of it either, really. But it's okay. Andrew is going to help. Once the bottles are found to be safe, because of *course* they will be, he'll work with the government officials to get your license sorted."

Her scowl darkened still further, and I was really afraid she was mad at me.

But then she just slumped over the table, like some animating force that had been possessing her had just left her body.

"Mormor?" I asked as she sat there with her face buried in her hands.

"I've let too much go for too long, haven't I?" she said, her voice muffled by her hands. "I thought I was managing well enough. That I would pick up the slack later when I had more energy. But that day just never came. Even though it always did before. And now this."

"Mormor," I said as soothingly as I could.

"No, Brigida isn't wrong. Dofri is dead in part because of me. I have to carry that guilt," she said. She dropped her hands and sat back in her chair, looking out my kitchen window with red-rimmed eyes.

"Forget about Brigida," I said. That wasn't the first suggestion to come to mind about what to do with Brigida, but my first impulse involved too many curse words. "You should get out of here."

"Yes, another walk," she said, but like an automaton. I could see that catatonia descending on her again. I got up from my chair and reached out to pull her out of hers.

"No, you need to get out of Villmark. If just for a little bit," I said. She was resisting me pulling her towards the front door, so I decided to try a different tack. "I need your help."

"For what?" she asked.

"I need to talk to Tuukka," I said. "I want to get the story straight from him about these property offers and who currently buys his honey. Come on. You were going for a walk, anyway. You might as well walk with me."

"Fine," she said.

She sounded grumpy, and her movements as she dressed for going outside were downright sullen. But I didn't mind.

I'd take it over that creepy lethargy any day.

# CHAPTER 13

*T*his time, when I walked up Tuukka's front step, I was going where I meant to. And even without my wand before my eyes, I had no trouble vividly imagining what his farm looked like at the height of summer. This was partly just remembering what I had seen with my wand that morning on Neil's property, but mostly it was older memories of the summer I had spent here as a child.

I was imagining the fields of clover so clearly I could almost smell the sweet pink and purple blossoms and hear the steady drone of the bees moving from flower to flower.

I really had to stop fantasizing about summer. I loved the winter!

But even people who loved the winter grew a little tired of it in mid-February, particularly a winter that went heavier on the wind and sub-zero temps than on deep drifts of snow.

I blinked myself back to reality and appreciate that even in winter, Tuukka's farm felt like a second home to me.

Especially when, after climbing the steps to the front door, my grandmother, as usual, just turned the knob and let herself inside.

"Tuukka?" she called as she pulled off her boots.

"Nora," he said as he emerged from the kitchen with a surprised smile. "What brings you here?"

"Ingrid," she said, then noticed I was still standing outside on the porch. "Come in, Ingrid. No sense leaving the door open."

I stepped inside. "Hello, Tuukka. Sorry if I'm a little distracted. I was just remembering what this place was like in the summer when I was little."

"Yes, not much to see in February," he said. "Would you two like some coffee?"

"Of course," my grandmother said, and followed him into the kitchen. I paused to remove my boots, looking around the tiny living room I was standing in as I struggled with the laces. Tuukka had never married. I would expect his house to look more like Neil's, with the ghost of his mother's presence lingering in some of the furniture choices, but no sense of a current feminine touch.

But Tuukka's furniture was only a few years old. There were no pastel colors or floral prints, but I still sensed a woman's opinion in the style choices. It all looked cozy, arranged around the fireplace as if ready for an old couple to sink into those comfortable chairs for a quiet evening at home after dinner.

The kitchen beyond was also on the small side, but as carefully arranged as a ship's galley. Everything needful was in easy reach, and yet there was no clutter. And even the floor was sparkling clean.

"I have some of that amaretto creamer in the fridge," Tuukka said as he watched my grandmother fill the basket of his coffeemaker.

"Still fresh?" she asked.

"Just bought it yesterday," he said.

"Lovely."

She moved towards the sink to fill the pot with water, and Tuukka slid easily out of her way. It was like they were short-order cooks used to working not just in tight spaces but with and around each other, intuitively knowing when one was going to turn away from the sink so the other could take mugs down from the cupboard.

Yep. The two of them definitely had a vibe. And that living room furniture, while thoroughly modern and not remotely like the hand-made wood items that my grandmother favored, was still very much to her taste.

"Do you come here a lot, mormor?" I asked.

She made a noncommittal sound, pretending to still be occupied with the coffeemaker. But Tuukka gave me a nervous smile.

"This time of year, I don't have fresh jars to bring to your grand-mother, you know. No reason to go to the hall. But she stops in to see me all the same."

"Speaking of honey, I was hoping you could bring over anything you have left in your stores," my grandmother said, finally turning away from the coffeemaker.

"Of course. I can pack it for you now if you like? Drive it over to the hall for you?"

"No, not just yet," she said, tapping a nail against the front of her teeth. "No, not just yet. I'll have to let you know when I'm ready for it. But I'll definitely need it."

"Did you lose a batch during fermentation?" he asked. "I don't think that's ever happened to you before."

"I did, through no fault of my own," she said. Then gave him an apologetic smile. "It's a long story."

"Oh, I see," he said. Then he turned to look at me. "What did you want to see me about, Ingrid?"

"I wanted to ask about the offers on your property," I said.

"Offers?" he repeated with a frown.

"Are you saying no one has offered to buy your farm?" I asked, almost alarmed at the thought. Was his memory going? Was he going to be of no use as a witness?

"No, I've had one offer," he said. "Young Neil next door made me a very good offer. But there was only the one, and I turned it down."

"May I ask why?"

"I'm just not ready," he said.

"This farm is a lot of work for you on your own," my grandmother said, almost sternly.

"Well, it wouldn't be just me on my own if you'd accept my propos-al," he said teasingly.

"Tuukka, hush," she admonished him.

He blushed ever so slightly, then cleared his throat. "Ingrid, yes, hmm. Where was I?"

"Neil offered to buy your farm, but you weren't ready," I said. "He told me all about it, actually. He wanted you to teach him your craft, and he was going to let you carry on living in the house. It sounded like a good deal. You'd have money on hand now when you could use it, but your life could carry on the same as it is now for as long as you like."

"Yes, he's a good boy. A good boy," Tuukka said. But he seemed to be speaking mostly to himself.

"Here," my grandmother said, handing each of us a mug of coffee. We sat down around the kitchen table, my grandmother stopping on the way to retrieve the creamer from the door of the refrigerator.

"I'm sorry to keep harping on this, Tuukka, but I understood that you had two offers?" I said.

He frowned into his mug. "For the farm? No. Just the one."

"You're forgetting about the second man," my grandmother said as she handed him the creamer. He poured a scant few drops into his coffee, and I almost laughed aloud. It couldn't be more obvious that he bought it for my grandmother, but was committed to pretending that amaretto was something that *he* liked.

He looked up at me with eyebrows raised, but I dodged his unspoken question. "Someone else came out here to the farm to offer to buy something, right?"

"Oh, that man," he said, nodding. "Yes, the strange fellow. He didn't want the farm itself, you see. Just the bees."

"Just the bees? Is that strange?" I asked.

"Well, he wasn't looking to acquire a few colonies. He wanted every single hive," Tuukka said. Then he frowned into his coffee again, as if it upset him somehow. "But the offer wasn't strange. The fellow was."

"Strange how?" I asked. "Was he dressed funny or speak with an accent or something?"

"He was dressed the same as anyone else. He *did* have a bit of an accent that I couldn't place for the life of me, but that wasn't it," he said. "You know, when people around here get visits from their cousins back in Norway or Sweden, they barely have an accent themselves. I suppose they learn from television."

I could see we were getting off topic. "Hold on," I said, digging into my art bag for my sketchbook. I grabbed the first pencil I touched, then drew out a hasty sketch of Dofri. Then I pushed it across the table to Tuukka. "Is this who you spoke to?"

"Yes, that's him," Tuukka said. "You know him?"

I didn't answer that. I just put the sketchbook away. "I'm guessing you said no to selling your bees."

"That's right. I would sooner take Neil's offer; I've known that boy since he was a baby. This strange fellow I knew not at all."

There was that word again. "Can you explain to me how he was strange? Take your time."

Tuukka stared out the window for a minute, absently rubbing at the point of his chin. I glanced over at my grandmother, but she just gave me the smallest of nods, a sign to wait quietly.

At last, Tuukka looked back at me and my grandmother. "The man with the slight accent, he understood bees. From what he said, I could tell that, unlike Neil, he wasn't going to need any help to get going. A natural beekeeper, as much as I can judge such a thing from one meeting. But a businessman he was not. And without a head for business, my bees would ultimately suffer in his care, I'm afraid."

"How could you tell he had no head for business?" I asked.

"He didn't understand the first thing I said when we started discussing money."

"You discussed money?" my grandmother asked with a stern glower.

"Only a bit," he assured her. "You know I wouldn't make any decisions without consulting you first. And I'd never sign anything you hadn't read. Nora, we agreed."

"So he brought up the money?" I guessed.

"He did, but he didn't seem to understand the words he was using,"

Tuukka said. "About bees, he spoke easily and naturally, but about money, it was like the words were foreign to him. Not just the words, the basic concepts. I already wasn't going to say yes, so it didn't matter. It's just an impression I got. I don't think it matters. It's just why I said he was strange."

"Okay," I said. "When did this happen? Before or after Neil approached you?"

"Oh, after. Well after," he said. "It was just last week."

"And he only came the one time?" I asked.

"So far," he said. "He felt like someone that would be persistent. Actually, I'm a bit surprised I haven't seen him again. I expected him to bone up on what he didn't get right the first time and to try me again. Not that I would say yes," he added with a glance at my grandmother.

She didn't return his look, but I had a hunch why Dofri had never come back. If I had my timeline correct, she had scared him off before he was even going to try.

I could kind of see why. Tuukka was clearly impressed by Dofri's knowledge of bees. If he had upped his business talking points and come back, would Tuukka have caved?

And if he had, would he have regretted it?

I would give decent odds the answer to both questions was yes. But clearly my grandmother thought it even more likely. And it was her place to look out for him.

I turned back to Tuukka. "Did it seem like the two of them were working together? Dofri and Neil?"

"Dofri? Is that the fellow's name?" he asked, but then shook his head. "No, I don't think they knew each other at all. Did they?"

"They did, I just don't know how well," I said.

"What's this all about?" he asked.

I opened my mouth to speak, but my grandmother quickly cut me off. "Nothing you need to worry yourself about, Tuukka. I'm handling it." I must've bristled at that remark because she hastily added, "well, Ingrid and I are handling it. Or, mostly Ingrid."

"Oh. Well, if you have more questions?" he said.

"Not now," I said. My grandmother was already getting up from the table to head for the door. I was in danger of being left behind. My grandmother always did move at top speed.

"Well, you're welcome anytime if anything else should pop up," he said and walked with us back to the front door.

"Does it get lonely out here, on the edge of Runde?" I asked him. "I hope Neil stops in to see you at least. He mentioned chores, but I hope he's occasionally a little more social than that."

"Oh, he does. He is. Sometimes, we have dinner together. When Nora isn't by, of course," he added.

My grandmother's cheeks flushed a rather lovely shade of pink. Which was totally unlike her.

"Of course," I said, smiling at Tuukka.

"It wouldn't get lonely at all if your grandmother would just say yes," he said. There was a mischievous gleam in his eye. He was deliberately provoking my grandmother. That was something very few people got away with.

Apparently not even Tuukka, as she straightened up and shot him a furious glare. "Stop speaking nonsense, Tuukka Jakanpoika, or I shall never darken your door again."

"Of course, herkkupeppu," he said to her, giving me a little wink.

"None of that!" my grandmother said, raising a finger as if in warning. "And in front of my granddaughter. Really!"

Then she stormed out of the house, marching back down the front walk at a speed closer to running than walking.

"Thanks for the coffee," I said to Tuukka.

But he caught my sleeve before I could head out the door, and when I turned back to look at him, his face was suddenly grave.

"Take care of your grandmother," he said. "I didn't ask about it because I know she'd never tell me what's wrong, but she doesn't look well at all."

"She's just tired," I assured him.

"It's more than tired," he said.

"You're right," I admitted. "She's staying with me now. At my place.

We came here now mostly because she needed an outing, and I think she wanted to see you."

He lit up at that, then dropped his eyes as if afraid I'd see what he was feeling there.

As if it weren't obvious in his whole demeanor.

But, alas, I was pretty sure it was never meant to be.

"Take care," I said, and hurried to catch up to my still fuming grandmother.

"What was that all about?" I asked. Then I noticed she had turned right on the road and not left, towards the rest of Runde. All that lay ahead of us were the bluffs. The unclimbable bluffs. "And where are we going?"

"Shortcut," she said, never breaking her stride.

"That's all you're going to say?" I asked. "Because I haven't seen you this angry since the last time you spoke with Frór."

She stopped so suddenly I kept going three more steps and had to turn and come back to her. But she didn't say anything. She just glowered at me.

"You didn't use to be this irritable, did you?" I asked. "I mean, I know Frór rubs you the wrong way. That's been true since as far back as I can remember. Which is further back than I could remember a month ago. But I've never seen you get this upset with Tuukka. He was only teasing you."

"You're right," she said, to my complete surprise. "Close your mouth. It may be the middle of February, but you can still catch flies with your jaw hanging open like that."

I shut my mouth, which had indeed been hanging open. "You're showing me your shortcut *and* telling me I'm right both in the same afternoon?"

"Don't get cute," she said, then started leading the way towards the bluffs again, but this time at a more walkable pace. "I'm showing you *a* shortcut. I have plenty of others that are still secret."

"I'm sorry. I shouldn't have brought up Frór. That wasn't appropriate," I said.

But she just sighed. "No, you're right. It's time the two of us talked about some things. Far past time. But let's get a little further out of Runde first."

"Okay," I said.

This time it was me keeping the brutal pace, even though I didn't know where we were going. I was that anxious to hear what my grandmother had to tell me.

# CHAPTER 14

$\mathcal{T}$he road ended abruptly where the bluffs rose up almost vertically. It certainly looked like a dead end to me. But somewhere under that untouched snow there must be a path, because my grandmother just kept walking.

It was too strenuous a climb for talking, even if there hadn't also been all that snow and ice to deal with. I still wasn't sure if we were following a path or if my grandmother was forging her own trail. I just followed a pace or two behind her, putting my boots in the marks left by her own feet.

We climbed the slope at an angle, but the switchback I was expecting never came. I looked down to my right and I could see the roof of Tuukka's farmhouse and, beyond it, Neil's.

Then I looked up past my grandmother. When I had realized we weren't climbing in a zig-zag up to the level of the highway, if several football fields further inland from the bridge, I had assumed we would end up in the cavern behind the waterfall.

But I realized now that that wasn't correct either. No, if we kept going in the direction she was heading, we'd reach the top of the waterfall itself. We'd be at the edge of the meadow that overlooked Runde, if further south than I had ever been in that meadow.

My grandmother kept climbing at a steady pace like a machine, but once we were on level ground, she stopped, resting her hands on her knees as she caught her breath.

"Are you all right?" I asked, barely able to get the words out myself. The muscles in my thighs were burning.

"Just need a minute," she said. Then she gave me a tired sort of smile. "It's nice to wear myself out with exercise for once and not magic, you know?"

"I'm guessing you don't come up this way a lot," I said.

"No," she agreed.

I waited for her to recover, but when she finally straightened up again, she turned to walk away.

"Hey, you were going to talk to me about something," I reminded her.

"Oh?" she said, as if she had no idea what I was talking about.

"Are you honestly going to make me bring Frór up again just to remind you?" I said.

"No," she said. She said nothing more, and was walking at a pretty quick pace for someone who had just made that steep climb.

"If you've changed your mind about talking to me, that's okay," I said, and tried not to sound as sullen as I felt.

"Let's talk about you first," she said, and finally slowed down to a more comfortable walk.

"Me? What does anything have to do with me?" I asked.

"I promise this will prove relevant. Indulge me," she said.

"Fine, but I'm still not clear on what you want me to tell you," I said.

"I want you to talk to me about Andrew and Thorbjorn," she said.

"Seriously?" I said and stopped walking. We were still among the beech trees, the edges of Villmark not yet in view even through the leafless limbs.

"I know things have been changing for you, even if I don't get to chat with you as much as I would like," she said. "Thorbjorn goes out on patrol all the time. But this time it seems to be bothering you."

"It's not like all the other times," I said. I was hugging my arms tight around myself even though after that walk I wasn't particularly cold.

"Frór and the Thors are being careful. I'm sure there is no more danger now than there's been before," she said.

"It feels like more," I said. "And after what happened with the Fe rune and how I accidentally summoned fire giants, it kind of feels like things might be my fault. At least partly."

"That's not the case," my grandmother said after a moment's thought. "You have your power under control now. And this nonsense with the artifacts turning up out of nowhere is definitely not on account of you."

"Maybe," I said, but I couldn't make myself believe that.

"But there's more to it than the possible danger," she said. "There's an unsettledness about you."

"Thorbjorn and I were having a conversation we didn't get to finish," I said.

"About?"

"The future, I guess?" I said. "Well, that and the past."

"Because you have your memory back," she said. I looked at her closely, but there was no hint she felt any guilt about that. Not that I wanted her to feel guilty.

Well, maybe I did, a little. It had been her spell that had taken my memory away, after all. And it wouldn't have been so potent if she had waited until she was less angry with Frór to cast it.

"When we were kids, we made plans," I said. "We intended to work together, side by side, volva and guardian. I didn't realize that was what Thorbjorn was always waiting for me to remember until, well, I remembered."

"Guardian is not an office the way volva is," my grandmother said with a little sniff.

"It's a calling. A responsibility. I think it's only more meaningful for being a bit more freely chosen than being a volva," I said.

"Being a volva is a choice," she said to me sternly. "A choice you have left to make, I might add."

"I know you say so, but surely you don't think I could come this far, let alone farther than I am now, and then choose to walk away?"

"I don't know what the future holds," she said.

"Well, that makes two of us," I said.

"So you didn't get to conclude your conversation with Thorbjorn about your roles in each other's lives and in Villmark," she said. "That would explain the unsettledness."

"Yes," I agreed. But there was more to it than that.

I couldn't stop remembering watching him and his brothers walk away, Kara beside me, also watching, her hand clutching mine so tightly.

"So what about Andrew, then?" she asked.

I blinked. "Andrew?"

"I saw the two of you together last night. The energy between you was, again, very disturbed."

I had no idea she spent so much time watching me, not just with normal eyes, but with magical ones as well, apparently.

"Actually, it was kind of the same problem between us," I said. "He is anxious for me to come back to Runde, but I don't know when that will even be possible. He's also had a job offer in Duluth, an important stepping stone for his career. I'm not sure he was exactly happy when I encouraged him to take it."

"No, I can see how that wouldn't be what he wanted to hear," my grandmother agreed. "But it was a kindness, I think, you telling him that."

"It didn't feel kind," I said. "It feels like slow cruelty, every time I talk to him. But the truth of the matter is that I'm not ready to make any major decisions. Not yet."

"You said you were already certain you wanted to be a volva," she pointed out.

"Yes, but I don't know what that will mean, do I? Does it mean I have to give up Runde? Or my career as an artist? It would have to be a part-time career, sure, but honestly, I always expected that to be true. I was going to have to do something to earn my keep until I made it as an artist. If that ever even happened. Not a lot has changed about that, really."

"And Thorbjorn?"

"Well, I can't commit to the sort of close working relationship he's envisioning if I'm planning to spend half my days in Runde, can I?" I asked.

"I think you were closer before, when you said you don't know what any of it will mean in the future," she said. "But in the meantime, not making promises you don't know if you'll be able to keep is the wisest course. In case you wanted my stamp of approval."

"It's always nice to have that," I said.

Then, without a word, we both just carried on walking through the trees to Villmark.

"Wait, you said this would all be relevant to what you had to tell me," I reminded her. "But I'm not seeing it. I mean, I'm not ready to make any major decisions, but surely the same can't be said of you."

To my surprise, my grandmother laughed out loud at that. She was laughing so hard she had to stop walking and put her hands on her knees again.

I just looked at her, dumbfounded, until she pulled herself together. She wiped tears from her eyes, then carried on walking.

"Mormor?" I prompted.

"Sorry," she said, still chuckling to herself. "Ingrid, sometimes you're never ready. I've lived more years than I'd care to count, but the decisions you're weighing now, I've never committed to one way or another myself."

"You didn't decide to live between Runde and Villmark?" I asked.

"I never made a declaration to do so, not even to myself," she said. "Some of that was about your mother. I was afraid I would lose her if I didn't keep a foot in the world she had fled to. But she wasn't all of it. Not by a longshot."

"I suppose if she had been the reason, that would've changed when she died and I came here to live," I said.

"I think I just got used to things as they are," she said.

"Living between the two worlds is draining you," I guessed.

She nodded and sighed. "Yes. The others think it's just the mead hall with all of its spell work. But trying to live with my heart in two places is just hard."

That hurt just to hear. I had secretly been hoping that when I was able to take over the mead hall, it would mean my grandmother would be able to rest and just enjoy life for a while. But now I could see that wasn't true. She would still be stretched out too thin. It wasn't about magic at all.

"So that's why you keep turning Tuukka down? Because you'd have to give up Villmark?" I asked.

"He doesn't even know it exists," she said. "I thought about telling him, I still do sometimes, but in the end I never do."

"But you pushed me to tell Andrew and the others," I said.

"Perhaps I have regrets on that score," she said. "It doesn't matter. I'm too old now to try cohabitating with anyone. I've never actually managed it with anyone but your mother, and now for bits of time with you."

"You don't seem like a tough housemate," I said.

"No, maybe not," she said. "Maybe I've just left it for too long. I can't tell him now. It would upend his entire life, and he doesn't deserve that. Especially if I know, as I do, that in the end I still wouldn't be able to give him the answer he wants. No, I'm just too set in my ways."

We were nearing the square in the center of the village, and I knew asking the question that was foremost in my mind was running the risk of getting snapped at again. But I just couldn't leave it alone.

"If Tuukka doesn't know about Villmark, then he doesn't know about Frór," I said. "That's the main thing, isn't it?"

"Very astute," she said with a frown. "But that's a whole other topic, one we'll have to table for now."

"Why?" I asked.

"Because that's Loke there, standing by your front gate with your cat," she said, pointing with one mittened hand up the road ahead of us. "And from the way he's pacing about, I'd say he has something he's dying to tell you."

Loke was indeed pacing furiously back and forth, head down and hands deep in his trouser pockets. Mjolner sat on the gatepost, tail wrapped primly around all four paws, his cat head swiveling back and forth, never losing eye contact with Loke.

Then Loke looked up and saw us approaching. He ran towards me, indeed very eager to speak to me.

"You never texted me back," I chided him, but he just waved that away.

"I was busy," he said.

"Doing what?" I asked.

"Finding your mystery woman," he said.

He beamed at me, clearly very pleased with himself.

But I couldn't help grinning back at him. I was pretty pleased with him, too.

Now I had a lead to followup on. I just hoped it would be a good one.

# CHAPTER 15

*T*his time when I found myself in the meadow over the waterfall, I was further north along its length than I had ever been before.

For someone who longed to make a life for herself where Runde and Villmark overlapped, I didn't know as much about those places as I ought to.

"I didn't know anyone lived this far east of Villmark," I said as Loke and I trudged through the snow. It wasn't an easy walk. The meadow grasses were like little tents of air under the cover of the snow, and the top layer was icy from the wind blowing off of Lake Superior.

Each step crunched through that ice and almost came to a rest in the snow. It felt like my foot was on solid ground, but the moment I put weight on it, it would crush through one of those air pockets, throwing me off balance.

I imagined it was worse for Loke, whose low-topped boots simply had to be filled with snow by now.

"Why are you never dressed for the weather?" I asked him.

"She's just up there, in that cottage. Do you see it?" he asked, effectively distracting me. I followed the direction of his pointing finger until I did indeed make out a rounded, snow-covered mound the size of a small house or large hut.

"What did you say her name was?" I asked.

"I didn't," he said. "It's Fasta. She's even more of a loner than your old friend Solvi."

"How do you know that?" I asked.

"Because almost no one knows her," Loke said. "I asked all over town and no one knew who I was talking about. Not until I got to the Freyas' bakery. They do some business with her on occasion. By which I mean two or three times a year."

"No one else knew her?" I asked, surprised. There just weren't that many people in Villmark. I had always assumed they all knew each other, if only by sight.

"Nope," Loke said.

"But the Freyas knew where she lived?" I asked.

"Their mother Jóra did," he said. "Apparently they are of an age."

"Like they went to school together?" I asked.

"Pretty much," he said.

We were reaching the edge of the meadow, and we could finally see signs of human life in the snow. There were footprints leading from the far side of the cottage where I presumed the front door to be. They circled around the back of the cottage, then headed towards the top of the bluffs.

But they ended at a series of snow-covered mounds, much smaller than the hut. They were also more squared-off. I think part of me was expecting what I found when we drew closer.

"Bee hives," I said, a little too excited. "She must get those hay bales from Runde. Can you make them square up here in Villmark?"

"Not really," Loke said. "I had no idea you were so into beekeeping."

"Don't you see? This can't be a coincidence," I said.

"I have no idea what you're talking about," he said.

As cold as the wind blowing in from the lake was, Loke seemed unbothered by it as he listened intently to me catching him up on what I'd learned so far about Tuukka and the offers on his farm.

"If Dofri was looking to get into mead production, this makes total sense, right?" I said.

"More than total sense," Loke said. "If he was hoping to sell this mead of his in Villmark, he'd be much better served using Villmarker honey. It matters to a lot of people."

"I think you're right," I said, but then I frowned. "So why do I get the sense that he only talked to Fasta after he'd given up hope on bringing Tuukka around?"

"I don't know. Let's go talk to her and see if we can figure that out," Loke said.

We went around to the front of the snug little cottage. It was nearly covered in snow, looking more like an oddly shaped hill than a habitation. But there was a chimney protruding from the top of it. I could smell wood smoke even though the wind was carrying it away too briskly to be seen billowing out the top.

The snow had been cleared away from the front of the house, revealing a tall but narrow door between two windows so frost-covered it was impossible to see a thing through them. Loke knocked briskly then stepped back, clearly eager to put his hand back in his pocket.

The door swung open. At first, it seemed to do this of its own accord, but then a tall woman stepped out of the shadow, clutching the edge of the door as she looked out at us.

At first I thought Loke had been wrong about her being the same age as Jóra. She looked too fit to be much older than us, more like the Mikkelsen sisters than Jóra or even Gunna. From what little I had learned of beekeeping from spending childhood days with Tuukka, it didn't build the sort of muscles I could see not just in her arms but all over her body.

She was also exceptionally tall, even for Villmark. I had the sudden thought that perhaps she was part giantess.

Then I realized I had no idea if that was even a thing that happened outside of fairy tales.

Well, it wasn't the most improbable story from a fairy tale book that I had discovered to be absolutely real in the last few months.

"Fasta?" Loke asked.

"Yes?" she said, taking another half-step outside. Now I could see that her dark blonde hair was shot through with strands of gray, and the skin of her face, especially around her dark blue eyes, was showing damage from a lifetime spent working in the sun.

"We were hoping to talk to you about Dofri," I said.

"About Dofri," she said. "Very well. Won't you come in?"

She retreated back into the shadows. Loke glanced at me and I went in first.

At first the space under that dome of snow felt cave-dark, but then as my eyes adjusted I decided what it really was was cozy. Clearly, only one person lived here, and she never had guests. There was a single bed against the far wall, and a single stool set close to the deep red embers of the banked fire in the belly of a cast-iron stove. But it had everything she could need, all within easy reach. I could see implements of cooking, spinning and weaving all neatly arranged in open boxes around that stool. There was even a drop spindle resting on the ground, as if she had set it down by her feet before coming to answer the door.

"Are we intruding?" I asked.

"Not at all," she said. There was just barely enough room for the three of us to press together so that she could swing the door shut again. "I don't often entertain guests. Please forgive me if my hospitality is rusty from disuse. Would you like some coffee?"

"That would be lovely," Loke said before I could demure. Well, he did look like he could use a hot drink.

"Please, feel free to sit on the bed," Fasta said as she set about spooning coffee into the central component of an old-fashioned flip coffee maker. She filled the bottom with water from a kettle sitting at the back of her stove, then flipped the whole thing over and left it to drip while she took a single tin mug out of the cupboard overhead and set it on her little table.

Then she bent over a bucket of water sitting on the floor and dug in the warm, soapy water for another matching mug. She rinsed it carefully with water from a second bucket, then dried it with a towel before setting it beside its mate.

Then she looked up at the two of us, watching her from the edge of the bed.

"Honey cakes?" she asked, holding out a tea-towel-lined basket filled with sticky, golden-colored hexagonal pastries. They had clearly been baked in some sort of mold: half were shaped like pieces of honeycomb and half were adorned with the outline of a bee in flight.

Their caramelly sweet aroma was irresistible. The outside was crispy like the honey-soaked crust of a slice of bread, but the inside was creamy-soft and still warm.

"Did you know we were coming?" Loke asked between nibbles of his own cake.

"No. In fact, I was expecting Dofri. But it appears something else has come up. I'm torn between thinking he's just running late or isn't going to turn up at all. I don't suppose you saw him on your way here?" She looked at us both as she waited for us to answer. She looked a bit unsure of herself, exactly like someone who wasn't used to company would look when finding herself accidentally entertaining guests she hadn't been expecting.

"Don't you know?" I asked.

"Don't I know what?" she asked as she poured out the coffee. "As I'm sure you know, I don't get out much. I was out last night to meet with Dofri, but he wasn't able to speak with me at the time. We arranged to meet here this morning, but he's nearly an hour late. Beyond that, no, I don't know anything."

"When did you leave the mead hall last night?" I asked.

She blinked as if surprised I knew where she had been. "I'm afraid I can't give you a time. I never bother with keeping track of such things."

"Was it before or after Dofri took a drink of his mead?" Loke asked.

"How would I know that?" she asked, confused. "He had a mug of mead with him. I have no idea when he drank from it."

"Not when you were with him, then?" Loke asked.

"How would I-?" she started to say. But then she stopped and gave it a moment's thought. "No, you're right. I did notice. I never saw him take a drink, but I assumed it was out of courtesy to me."

"What do you mean?" I asked.

"Well, Nora Torfudottir's mead is made from outsider honey," Fasta said. "Inferior honey. And since Dofri and I were meeting to discuss my superior honey... well, drinking it in front of me might have struck him as... not the thing to do."

I could see she was choosing her words carefully, but not carefully enough, to judge by the hot blood suddenly rushing through my ears.

"We didn't introduce ourselves," Loke said to me, then turned to Fasta. "Pardon our rudeness. We don't have your excuse of being rusty with this, and now it might seem like we were withholding our identities from you."

"I won't ascribe ill intent if you tell me it was an innocent mistake," she said, but I could see his words were putting her on edge. Her eyes were narrower now, as if she were growing suspicious of both of us.

"I'm Ingrid Torfudottir," I said. "Nora is my grandmother."

"Oh," she said, and her cheeks colored, but so slightly it was almost imperceptible in the dusky light of her home.

"And I'm Loke Grímsson," he said, putting out a hand. She took it almost absentmindedly.

Then she seemed to come to a decision. She looked to me again and said, "I do not regret any of my words. They were my honest assessment and I stand behind them."

"Fair enough," I said. There was certainly room enough in Villmark for more than one maker of mead, especially given the variety of mead halls providing the market for that product.

"So Dofri was speaking to you about buying your honey," Loke said as he reached for another honey cake.

"I believe that was what he intended," Fasta said. "Our discussions never quite got that far."

"Really?" I said.

"Really," she said firmly. "Why do you sound so skeptical?"

"I'm not skeptical," I said. "Are you aware that he was talking to other beekeepers about buying their stock? By which I don't mean the honey alone but the hives themselves?"

"The only other beekeepers in Villmark are Snorri and his sons," Fasta said. "I don't believe Snorri would sell a single hive, as he intends to divide it all between his four sons when he retires."

"Dofri was making inquiries outside of Villmark," I said.

Now her eyes narrowed, not in suspicion but in anger. "In Runde?"

"Yes," I said.

"He was talking to you?"

"Not me," I said.

"Ingrid lives in Villmark now," Loke said.

"That's not important," I said.

But Fasta had put it together on her own. "He was talking to that Finn?"

"Tuukka Jakanpoika," I said. "You know him?"

"I can see his property from the other end of the meadow," she said. "I'm aware of him."

"Well, you'd have to be, wouldn't you?" Loke asked as he licked the last of the crumbs off his fingers. "If you know for a fact your honey is superior, you must've tried his at some point."

"I have," she said. "So that's why Dofri isn't here now? Because he's doing business with an outsider instead of with me?"

That struck me as deeply ironic. Tuukka was far more plugged in to his own community than Fasta was with hers.

Of course that wasn't what she meant by outsider.

"I don't know what he was intending to do," I said. "I'm afraid he died last night."

"What? When?" she asked. Again, I didn't think her shock was feigned.

But Loke just had to say, "pretty much the moment you stepped out of the hall, right? When he drank the inferior mead?"

"You don't think I...?" But she couldn't bring herself to finish her own question.

"You seem pretty steamed up at the idea that Dofri was going to work with outsiders," Loke said with a shrug. "Imagine if he had told you himself, last night."

"But he didn't," Fasta said earnestly.

"I believe you," I said before Loke could goad her again. "But if there's anything you can remember about last night that might help us? You *were* the last person we know who spoke to him."

She sat quietly with her eyes closed, as if casting back in her mind. "He was abrupt. We had agreed to meet there. He had wanted to meet there; I don't know why. But when I got there, he was already very agitated. I don't know why; I didn't ask. He suggested meeting today, and I agreed. Happily. I wished we had just met here in the first place. Mead halls are always so crowded and so noisy."

"And you're sure you didn't see him drink his mead?" I asked. She shook her head. "Did he ever set it down anywhere?"

"You mean where someone else might get to it?" Fasta asked. "No, I don't think so. I think he had it in his hand the entire time. Yes, he kept bringing it up to his lips to take a sip but then remembering himself and lowering it again, untasted. As I said, I assumed that was out of deference to me."

"It sounds like you're probably right about that," I said.

"So you think it was poison," she said to me. "Again."

"Again?" I frowned at her, but Loke understood her.

"You mean like with Lisa," he said.

"Lisa? Was that her name? The woman Halldis poisoned last autumn? Wait, I did hear the name Lisa..." she trailed off, but then there was a look on her face like something had just clicked into place in her mind. "Well, that explains that."

"What explains what?" I asked.

"Oh, just that I was wondering why the other young man who was here was talking to me about what sorts of things could potentially kill someone but be completely masked by the sweetness of mead," she said. "Not my area at all, as I told him. The women who work in the restricted parts of the greenhouse are really the ones to ask about that. But he mentioned Lisa."

"Who was here?" I asked. But I was also wondering how they had approached the cottage. There had been no signs of other footprints in the snow on the meadow. So had they come from the woods? Where most Villmarkers didn't dare to go, especially now with the Thors so very far afield?

"What was his name?" she asked herself, steepling her fingers and tapping them on the front of her lips.

"Roarr?" I ventured.

"Yes, that was it. Roarr," she agreed.

Loke shot me a puzzled glance. I had left that detail out of my hasty retelling before we'd knocked on the door.

"Roarr," I said, with a bit more venom than I had intended.

"It does seem odd that he came to call," Loke said, his eyes shifting from me to Fasta and back again.

"Not just here," I said. "He spoke with my grandmother first. And with Neil Nilssen down in Runde before that. For all I know, he's even been talking to Tuukka. I certainly wouldn't be surprised."

"But he wasn't even there last night," Loke said. "And what does Roarr care about the mead trade?"

"My grandmother thinks he might be settling on some sort of work decision," I said.

"You don't sound like you believe it," Loke said.

"Not remotely," I said. "I should go find him. I want an explanation."

"Did we have more questions while we were here?" he asked, and I realized that Fasta was just staring at the two of us, clearly not following a bit of what we were saying.

"I don't think so," I said. "No, I think we're done here."

"Thank you most kindly for the coffee and cakes," Loke said. At least one of the three of us could remember his manners. "They really were the most fantastic cakes."

"Take another for the road," Fasta said, holding out the basket again. I mentally replaced the cakes Loke and I had taken, and the resulting image had a few holes in it. Like two or three cakes had already been eaten before we knocked on the door.

And they had still been warm. We had just missed him.

Then I remembered this was the second time in a day I had watched someone wash a coffee mug that Roarr had left behind. I felt like smacking myself on the forehead.

Instead, I gritted out a, "yes, thank you, Fasta."

"Wait," she said, and spun around to dig down into an open chest behind her. She emerged with a single jar filled with dark golden honey, a large slice of comb in the heart of the glass container. "Take this. It's for you. Try it and this Tuukka's honey together and see if you don't agree with me."

"Sure," I said, and tucked the jar into my art bag. Not that I didn't have better things to do with my time than blind taste test jars of honey, but I'd been rude enough for one day.

Well, I had been rude enough to Fasta, at any rate. As Loke and I tromped back through the snow, I was pretty sure I still had a little rude left to spend.

Just as soon as I caught up with Roarr.

# CHAPTER 16

*R*oarr wasn't at his house, and his parents had no clue where he might be. I had started there first because it was easiest, but I wasn't exactly surprised that it didn't lead anywhere.

Then Loke and I checked Ullr's hall. It was almost entirely empty, being so early in the day. Ullr and his wait staff told us they hadn't seen Roarr in quite some time. Again, this was pretty much what I expected to hear.

Loke had a few more ideas of places we could check, but each of them turned up no sign of Roarr, and no one we spoke to had seen him that day.

"He's probably back in Runde, don't you think?" Loke said to me.

I threw up my hands. I had no idea where else in Villmark to look, so we might as well head back down to Runde.

When we reached the cave, Kara was awake and sitting by the bonfire while her sister was catching a nap. She was certain that no one had passed through except me all day. But that didn't mean much. There were other paths between the two towns, and Roarr knew at least a few of them.

"Where to first?" Loke asked as we followed the path that ended behind the mead hall.

"I guess the hall," I said with a sigh.

"You don't think he'll be there," Loke guessed.

"No, I really don't," I said. "He's been a step ahead of me this entire investigation. Unless he has information that I don't that would prompt him to search the hall again, I don't think we're going to find him there. But it's the closest thing. We might as well check."

I unlocked the back door, and we both stepped inside. With all the lights out, the details of the room were obscured in shadows, but nothing had changed since I'd been there last. There was still police tape across the front door, and a stained patch on the floor where Dofri had fallen and spilled his mead.

"He might've come in here to investigate the crime scene," Loke said.

"Not without a key, and there's no sign of a break-in," I said.

"You said that he's been one step ahead of you all day. What was going to be your next step?" he asked.

"Check in with Andrew," I said and pulled out my phone. It only took a second for him to answer my text. "No news yet," I said.

"They're searching all possible poisons?" Loke asked.

"Yeah, Andrew told them it might be related to Lisa's death, so they're checking everything," I said.

"Do you think it is?" he asked.

"Related to Lisa? I don't see how that could possibly be true," I said.

"Maybe Roarr is up in Villmark questioning the women who work in the dangerous plant section of the greenhouse," Loke said.

"They won't know anything," I said. Loke raised his eyebrows at me as if doubting my certainty. "Everyone in Villmark knows what happened to Dofri. If they had any suspicions, they would've come forward with them already. Maybe after the medical examiner determines what poison was used, we'll have questions to ask them, but right now we just don't."

"So what do you want to do?"

I pondered the question. "I think I want to talk to Mandy Carlsen."

"You talked to her last night," Loke said.

"I did, but we were interrupted," I said.

"You think she's a suspect?"

"No, I don't think so. This feels like murder over a business deal gone wrong to me, only Mandy had nothing to do with any of that."

"But she was at the table with Dofri and Neil," Loke said.

"So she might know more about what they were discussing, I hope," I said.

"I thought Dofri left the table when Mandy arrived?"

"Not instantaneously," I said. "Just because it wasn't long when all three were there together doesn't mean something significant didn't happen."

"Okay, so, let's go see Mandy, then," Loke said. "If we hurry, we might catch Roarr."

"Nice," I said to him. "Do you know where she lives?"

"No. You?"

"No. With her parents, whose names I don't know. I've checked. There are a lot of Carlsens in the area," I said.

"For that matter, does she even live in Runde?"

"Yeah, sure, compound the difficulty why don't you?" I said.

Loke just shrugged.

Then there was a knock on the Runde door.

"Is that police tape just on the inside?" Loke asked, pointing to the yellow X across the double doors.

"No, both sides," I said. I had no idea who could be knocking on a building that was supposed to be empty. Were the police back? It certainly wasn't Andrew, who was still at the hospital.

I crossed the room and carefully untaped the X from the door, letting it fall to the floor before swinging one of the doors open.

It was Tuukka. His face lit up when he saw me.

"Ah, Ingrid. I was hoping I'd catch you here," he said.

"The hall is closed. I don't know for how long," I said. Then I remembered his conversation with my grandmother. "You didn't bring the honey now, did you? Because mormor asked you to hold on to it for now."

"No, I didn't bring the whole shipment. Just a single jar," he said, and pulled the jar in question out from behind his back. He held it out to me with a flourish.

"One jar? Why?" I asked.

"Just for you," he said. "I should've given it to you when you were out at the farm. It's been ages since you've tasted any of my honey. I just want you to remember that it's the best."

"Thanks," I said, tucking the jar into my art bag. Right next to the similar jar that Fasta had forced on me. It was almost like he knew that had happened. "Tuukka, has anyone else been to see you since my grandmother and I left?"

"Not the police or anything," he said.

"What about a young man about my age, tall with a trucker cap?" I asked.

"Oh, Roarr. Yes, Roarr stopped by," Tuukka said.

"And he was asking you questions about the farm?" I asked.

"Just about the honey, really. He asked if he could have a jar to try, and when I went to get it, I realized I should bring one to you as well," he said.

"Did he say why?" I asked.

"Just to taste it, he said," Tuukka said. "He'd heard it was the best on the North Shore."

"So he just took the honey and left?" I asked.

"Yes, that's right."

"Did he say where he was going next?"

"I didn't ask," Tuukka said.

"Okay. Well, thanks," I said.

He nodded, then walked back to where he had left his battered old pickup parked in the lot.

"What was that all about?" Loke asked. He was leaning against the bar, and I walked over to him and set my bag down on the stool between us. The two jars clanked together.

I had never wanted honey less in my life than I did in that moment.

"We should do this properly," Loke said, taking the two jars out of the bag and setting them side by side on the bar. Then he dropped down until his eyes were level with the jars, as if studying their color. Which, given how dim it was inside the unlit hall, was pretty much impossible. "We should get a panel together. Say, six people. Everyone tries a little of each. Blind taste test! That's what I'm thinking."

I said nothing. I just wandered around the room, blinking my eyes between the mundane world and the magical one. They were looking one and the same to me. I could occasionally see the mead hall, but even then the walls were normal logs. There was no magic left in this place.

Something tickled my cheek. I wiped it away with the heel of my hand, but it was just replaced by another tickle.

And my hand was wet.

Damn it. I was crying.

"Hey, Ingy," Loke said as I stopped in the middle of the room and tried to get myself back under control.

"Sorry. This just all feels so unnatural. Impossible, even. That all the spells are gone. They were so old, so tightly woven together," I said.

"You'll get it all back to rights as soon as Nora is up to it. I have no doubt about that," he said.

"Well, and that's the other part of it," I said, wiping at my face again. "What if she's never better? What if this has been a long time coming? What if I'm too late getting here to learn all this volva stuff to help her?"

"I don't believe that," Loke said. "Not of either of you. Nora still has decades left in her, and you're far more advanced in your studies than you give yourself credit for."

"I'm really not," I said.

He scoffed at me. "Please. I was here when you fixed the spells. I saw what you did."

"But it still all fell apart," I said.

"It went down because your grandmother needed to pull all that magic back to her," Loke said.

"You saw that?" I asked. Which made no sense. He hadn't even still been there.

CATE MARTIN

"I know that's what happened. The council made their decision, and the mead hall didn't need the magic anymore. Not as much as she did, anyway. Perhaps she intends to just put it all back again when she returns."

"I don't think that's how it works," I said. But I didn't really know, did I? I had no idea what the scope or limits of my grandmother's power was.

"Look, text Andrew, Jessica and Michelle," Loke said. "Get them working on finding out where Mandy Carlsen lives."

"That's a good idea," I said and scrolled through my phone for our group text so I could ask them all at once.

"That might take a while, so what should we do in the meantime?" Loke asked.

"I don't want to sit here eating honey," I said as I typed with my thumbs.

"Of course not," he said. "That was just an attempt to lighten the mood. I could see you were getting upset. But that was a total failure, wasn't it? My bad. Now, what can I do for you? Any task at all. Just name it."

I looked up at the ceiling, the perfectly mundane ceiling with its broken, discolored tiles and fluorescent light panels. They were dark, but I could see darker shapes here and there resting on the plastic. Dead bugs, probably.

Should I ask Loke to use his own brand of magic to put the hall back to rights?

I really wanted to see it as it should be as soon as possible, but doing it without my grandmother felt very wrong.

I could ask him to contact Thorbjorn. He said he could do it.

But only in dire need, I reminded myself. And me feeling blue wasn't remotely that.

"Keep up the Roarr hunt," I said. "Maybe you'll have more luck without me."

"I doubt that," Loke said. But then he gave me a deep bow and said, "your wish is my command. When next I see you, I'll have Roarr by the ear."

140

"Right," I said.

Loke went out the Runde door.

I sat down at the bar and took out my sketchbook. The two jars were still sitting there side by side in the gloom of the darkened room. But that very much matched my mood.

Twenty minutes later I had a very dark, graphite-heavy picture of two objects that might just be jars of honey. But there were no clues in that picture, just an overwhelming sense of doom.

I put the sketchbook and pencils away, then added both jars of honey. Everyone had responded to my text, but no one knew where Mandy lived. Michelle was going to check with her mother, but she hadn't texted an update since then.

I had a sudden urge to check on my grandmother again. But that meant going back up to Villmark.

Well, it wasn't like I had anything more important to be doing. And perhaps a walk would clear my head.

It was only when I found myself halfway across the highway bridge that I realized I was heading for my grandmother's shortcut behind Tuukka's farm and not the far shorter route behind the mead hall. Apparently, my autopilot really wanted to take the long way.

Or my intuition was trying to tell me something.

I hurried my steps.

# CHAPTER 17

*J* had thought my intuition was sending back to Tuukka for some reason, but as I made the turn onto the dead end road he lived on, I realized it must've been something else.

Because I could see Mandy Carlsen herself slamming shut Neil's front door and charging down his porch steps. I called out to her, but she didn't seem to hear me. I was at a full run, the jars in the bag bouncing on my hip clanging alarmingly together, but before I reached the driveway, she was in her car and backing out at high speed.

It was like she didn't even see me. She nearly clipped me as she slammed her car into drive and took off like a dragster, spraying me with snow and gravel before disappearing down the road towards the highway.

I only caught a brief glimpse of her face as she sped away. She looked like she had been crying, but something struck me as false with that. Like she had been pretending to cry?

She was clearly very upset, but I couldn't tell if that was anger or grief distorting her features. The flush of color to her cheeks made me inclined to say anger.

Well, that and the slamming of doors.

I brushed the snow and gravel off myself, then walked up Neil's porch steps to knock on his door.

He flung the door open, mouth already open to start yelling. Unlike with Mandy, I had no trouble reading his emotions. That was definitely anger turning his whole face red. When he saw it was me standing there and not Mandy, he shut his mouth and ran a hand down his face. In an instant, he was calmer. But from the dark slant of his brows, not particularly happy to see me.

"Hi, Neil. Again," I said, and to my horror, actually gave him a ridiculous little wave. I pulled the offending hand behind my back. He was not amused.

"What is it?" he gritted out.

"I had some questions."

"More questions?"

"About Mandy," I said.

He glowered at me. But then he stepped back, leaving the door hanging wide open. "Come on in," he said with forced cheeriness. "There is nothing I would love better than to tell you everything you could ever want to know about Mandy Carlsen."

His voice was dripping with sarcasm. But the door was still wide open. I suspected he meant it. He *did* want to tell me everything.

"Great," I said, stepping inside and closing the door. I set my bag on the floor, then slipped out of my boots before joining him in the kitchen. "You know, I've been wanting to talk to Mandy all day. I haven't been able to figure out where she lives."

"With her parents," Neil said as he filled two mugs from the coffeemaker.

I was really all coffee-d out, but I didn't mention that to him. Instead I said, "yes, but there are actually quite a few Carlsens in the area."

"There are, for whatever that's worth," he said, then turned to thump the mugs down heavily on the table, sloshing the contents over the rims.

"I don't follow you," I said. When it became clear that he wasn't going to move from where he was now standing against his counter, I reached past him and snagged his roll of paper towels. I pulled off a few squares, then gently sopped up the spilled coffee.

A little of the annoyance seeped out of his tone as he said, "Carlsen is her married name."

"Oh. I didn't even realize she was married," I said.

"Separated," he corrected me. "And he wasn't from here, so none of those Carlsens would've been any help to you."

"I guess I'm glad I didn't bother them, then," I said, looking around for the trash. He pushed off the counter to open the cabinet door under the sink behind him. The trash can was nestled in there next to a plastic caddy full of cleaning supplies. I tossed in the damp paper towels.

I straightened up to find Neil now sitting calmly at the kitchen table, sipping at his mug of coffee. I sat down across from him and clutched my own mug in my hands. The warmth was nice after being outside, even if I had no desire to drink any of it.

"Mandy is the little sister of my best friend from high school," he said, his eyes gazing down into his mug fixedly, as if he could see images from his high school days reflected there. "Greg and I knew each other since kindergarten, but we really bonded in high school. I spent as much time over at his house as I ever did here at mine. I was an only child, you know. And was born quite late in my parents' lives. It was lonely on the farm. But it was nice at Greg's house. His parents were young and interesting, always willing to drive us anywhere, and then after we could drive, they always let Greg take the car. They were kind of perfect."

"Sounds like it," I said. My high school days weren't so far behind me that I couldn't remember what a boon having a cool parent could be. My mother had always been ill, chronically ill, and often tired as well.

But she had also always been cool.

"The downside was Mandy. Wow, did she not seem like she came from the same parents as Greg. Her whole personality was so unlike the rest of them."

"In what way?" I asked.

145

"In every way," he said, and took a gulp of coffee. "She's like an emotional vampire. That's the only way to explain it. She thrives on drama, and if she's not getting it, she creates it. And she's very, very good at creating drama."

"That sounds exhausting," I said with unfeigned sympathy.

"Yeah. It's been nice the last few years. She married that Carlsen fellow. Mike, I think? They met in a bar on the Gunflint Trail while out snowmobiling. He was from the Iron Range. I want to say Virginia? They were married within a matter of months, and then she was gone. That wedding was a nightmare for Greg and his parents, though. Whew!" he said. "Bridezilla."

I could feel a whole irrelevant story coming on, and decided to head him off. "She's just now back in town, then? Because she's separated?"

"Yeah, it's only been a few weeks. But believe me, she's not going to wait for the divorce to be final before she starts spinning up more drama. She can't help herself. She's changed not at all."

"You mean she's dating?" I asked.

He barked out a laugh. "No, not yet. Not for lack of trying. Perhaps for lack of picking the right target for her attentions."

"What do you mean?" I asked.

"She's been trying to chase me," he said with another humorless laugh. "I've never liked her. She knew this. But she seemed to think if she were persistent enough, she could turn me around."

"You're using the past tense," I said.

"Yeah. About a week and a half ago, I got a little too brutally honest with her. She sulked for a couple of days, but then she was back again."

"Chasing you?"

"No, just hanging around where she knew I would be."

"Why?"

He chuckled again, but then his face just fell. "She knew the only place she'd find Dofri was in my company. That's why."

"So she was with you at the hall last night, but she was waiting to see Dofri?" I asked.

"No, she wasn't *with* me," he said with annoyance.

"Right, sorry. You were there with Dofri and she approached your table. Then Dofri left, right?"

"Pretty much," he said.

"You were still with Mandy when I asked you questions," I said.

"I wasn't *with*-"

"Got it," I said, holding up a hand to silence his protest. "Sorry. But you were standing near her. And you kept looking at her when you were answering my questions. Why?"

"As much as she drives me crazy, she's still my best friend's kid sister. I guess I can't help trying to look out for her. Try to keep her from getting herself into trouble."

"What did you think she was going to do?" I asked.

"The truth? I really thought she was going to convince you that I had done something. Make up some story. Just to get back at me for what I said to her before."

"Revenge is her kind of thing?" I asked.

"Revenge is totally her kind of thing," he said. "Pitting people against each other is her favorite method of getting revenge. If I didn't want her, and Dofri didn't want her, what better way to get back at us than to poison our relationship."

An ironic choice of words, under the circumstances. Or maybe a Freudian slip. "Did she succeed at it? You said you were talking about doing business together, but that fell apart. Was Mandy to blame?"

"I don't think so. Unless she was whispering in Dofri's ear, turning him against me. But I don't see that happening. He would not tolerate being alone with her, I'm sure of that."

"Did he tell you why he wasn't going to do business with you?" I asked.

"He said that upon reflection, he had decided that the entire matter would simply be too complicated. Which I don't get at all. How would me buying Tuukka's farm and then selling him honey be too complicated?"

I was pretty sure I understood what Dofri meant. Not that I could explain it to Neil.

"That was last night he told you this?" I asked.

"Yeah. I was still trying to talk him around when Mandy showed up. She was in rare form the minute she walked up to us."

"Angry?" I asked.

"Not at all. More like she was thinking she had her seduction settings cranked to the max. Which didn't work on either of us. Especially not on Dofri. He's a pretty withdrawn guy. He didn't like the attention she was attracting."

"And so then things turned sour?" I asked.

"They already were sour," he said. "Dofri had reached the point of brutal honesty much faster than I did. It was a couple of days ago. I don't know exactly what he said to her, but for a couple of days there, we had peace and quiet. We could conduct our business in peace. That was the most annoying part of it, really. If Dofri had been just a friend, we could've laughed Mandy off together. But he wasn't a friend. He was an acquaintance I was trying to talk business with. Her behavior was beyond annoying."

"So everything between you and Dofri was fine until Mandy showed up again last night?" I guessed.

"Fine?" He frowned to himself. "Like I said, our negotiations weren't going the way I'd have liked, but at least we were still talking. And were able to talk to each other without interruption."

"So Mandy was hitting on Dofri," I said. "What happened then?"

Neil sighed and rubbed at the back of his neck. "She was crazier than usual. She was trying to make a play at me to make him jealous. It was just awkward for all of us."

"Probably just for two of you," I said, and he laughed.

"Right. For two of us," he agreed. "And for everyone around us who could hear what was going on. But Dofri got fed up pretty quickly. He gave us some pretext about having to talk to someone on the far side of the room, and then he was gone."

"I don't think that was a pretext, actually," I said. "Maybe a happy coincidence, though. I do know he was meeting someone, but he only spoke with her long enough to reschedule their talk."

"Whatever," Neil said with a shrug, and drained the last of his coffee.

"So why was Mandy here now?" I asked. "Is she looking to buy hives or farms as well?"

"Mandy?" he said, almost choking on his coffee. "No way. Farming is definitely not the life for Mandy."

"Well, if she was coming around here to try to hook up with you..." I trailed off, rolling one hand to imply the rest of my sentence.

"Yeah, I know," he said. "She doesn't want to be a farmer's wife, either. I'm sure her intent is to run me to ground first, and then get to work changing everything about my life to suit her needs. Her ex has my deepest sympathies."

"So why was she here just now?" I asked.

"Just to make trouble," he said, but then cut me off before I could ask that question a third time. "Her pretext was to ask me about Dofri. What I thought happened to him, if the police are involved, what you may or may not know."

"She brought up me?" I asked, surprised.

"No, I did when she wanted to know who was looking into things," he said.

"She doesn't know who I am," I guessed.

"She knows Nora. By extension, she knows who you are. She knows not to mess with you, for sure," he said.

"So you think she was only pretending to be curious about Dofri's murder investigation? You think it was really about getting to you again?" I asked.

He got up to take his mug to the sink, but glanced over his shoulder to look at me. "You sound like you doubt that."

"Maybe it's the other way around," I said. "Maybe she wants to know what's going on, but she decided to ask you because you'd assume she had a different motive."

"But why would she care about the investigation?" he asked as he set his mug in the sink. Then he gripped the sides of the counter as if to steady himself. "Wait, are you saying she thinks you're investigating *her*?"

"Did it feel like that might be true when she was talking to you?" I asked. "I wasn't here. I'm relying on your impressions on this."

"I don't know," he said, too quickly. He wasn't even trying to recall. "Why would she think you were investigating her?"

"Guilty conscience?" I said.

"Wait, you think she's a suspect?" he asked.

"Is it possible?" I asked. "Would murder be part of creating drama? Maybe even something she hoped would bring the two of you closer? She certainly could have come here with two agendas."

"I just don't think so," he said. "If anything, she would've latched onto a third guy and put him up to it on her behalf. Getting her own hands dirty? I don't think so. No, not Mandy."

He was still leaning against the counter, arms crossed and shoulders scrunched up as if he were trying to disappear from my sight. He was looking down at his feet, but he glanced up at me just for a fraction of a second.

I was pretty sure he thought it was at least possible for Mandy to kill someone.

But if he thought she had, if everything he'd seen over the past days and weeks added up to anything like her being that driven, that crazy, he didn't say so.

Which, considering everything else he had been saying about her, meant something. He was the last person to try to protect her or shield her from an investigation. If she had killed Dofri for scorning her, he could very well be next. He must be thinking that, the same as I was. If he thought she was guilty, he would be throwing her at me. I was sure of that.

"Right," I said, pushing the mug of cooled coffee away. "Can you tell me where she lives?"

"I can tell you where her parents live, but I don't think you'll find her there. At least, not now," he said.

I only half heard his words because something on the kitchen table had caught my eye the moment I had leaned forward to stand up from my chair. I hovered there, hands on the table, butt hovering over the seat of my chair, slowing moving up and down until I saw it again.

There, a small array of spilled sugar scattered over the table next to my mug. The last person to sit here and drink coffee had dispensed it too hastily or with too shaky a hand.

But the glittering crystals weren't randomly dispersed like a starscape. They were arranged exactly like the rune thurs.

Or, more specifically, an inverted thurs.

"Chaos," I whispered to myself. A chill ran up my spine.

"What's that?" he asked.

"Nothing. What were you saying?" I asked, as I finally stood all the way up.

"Just that Mandy wasn't going home from here," he said.

"Where was she going?" I asked.

"To see Nora."

"But my grandmother isn't home. She's at my house," I said.

"Well, apparently not at the moment," Neil said. "Mandy was in the middle of one of her scenes here with me, pretending to be so distraught over poor Dofri, when her phone buzzed. I saw the text."

"From my grandmother?" I said incredulously. I had given her a cellphone for Christmas, but so far as I knew she had never even taken it out of the box.

"It said Nora on the text and the contact info both. Your grand-mother was agreeing to meet her at her house. They must both be there now. That threw Mandy off her groove, for sure. She tried to keep up the grieving act, but I wasn't buying it. The rest of our conversation was very much less in her control."

"Right," I said. My fear of not being able to get any information out of Neil was turning into the opposite problem.

I wasn't going to be able to shut him up. I could see him collecting his thoughts, ready to launch into a recreation of whatever had led up to the moment I had witnessed with Mandy slamming the door on her way out.

And it might even be relevant.

But it wasn't the time for it. My instincts were screaming at me that my grandmother was walking blindly into danger. I had to get there, fast.

"Text my grandmother," I yelled to Neil as I ran to the front door and shoved my feet back into my boots. "Tell her I'm on my way, but to absolutely not be alone with Mandy. Do it!"

"I will. I am now," Neil said, so flustered he nearly dropped his phone, pulling it out of his pocket.

"Then text Andrew and Jessica and Michelle and Luke," I said, putting my art bag's strap over my shoulder and head until it rested across my body.

"I don't know those people," Neil said, even as his thumbs were flying. "Wait, Andrew Swanson?"

"Yes!" I said, already out the door. He came out onto the porch in his stocking feet.

"What do you want me to tell him?"

"Tell him my grandmother is in danger. Tell him to tell everyone," I said.

And then I ran.

I just hoped I wasn't already too late.

# CHAPTER 18

*W*hen I first learned that my grandmother was a volva, and that I too had a calling to be a volva, I confess I didn't exactly understand what that would mean. I knew volvas were something like witches, seeresses who would use magic for divination so they could advise rulers.

Working by my grandmother's side, I had refined that vague idea into something more concrete. Being a volva in Villmark meant being a judge when needed, a protector of the village from bad magics, a general kind ear for anyone who needed to speak from their hearts, and yes, an adviser to the council.

What I had been slower to recognize was just how much running was involved. But after the last few days, I couldn't deny that I spent a lot of time running, running as fast as I could.

In hiking boots. And a parka. With a heavy bag bouncing on my hip.

At least this time I was on plowed roads and not struggling through snow drifts in the middle of the forest.

I reached the level of the highway before I absolutely had to slow down. My vision was starting to erupt in black starbursts, and if I didn't get my wind back, I just knew I was going to faint.

But I didn't want to stop. I managed to keep up a respectable jog as I crossed the bridge back towards the north end of Runde.

Jogging left my mind too free to fret, though.

Just why was I so sure that Mandy was a threat to my grandmother? If I were being honest, it wasn't exactly logical. Neil had been rather intensely stalked by her for weeks and still didn't think of her as more than an annoyance.

I cast my mind back to the night before, when I had spoken with her myself. She had not radiated any kind of menace at all. I could certainly see why Neil found her annoying, but nothing about her had seemed remotely dangerous.

I knew from experience that when I studied a new rune, I tended to see it everywhere. The inverse thurs that appeared in the sugar spill might just be my brain finding patterns where there weren't any.

But I didn't think so. I could form too clear an image in my head of Mandy deliberately spilling sugar from her spoon. Maybe even arranging it with a fingertip?

I almost stopped running all together, so vivid was that picture in my head. If it were true, it would mean so many improbable things were also true. Like Mandy knew what runes were and how to use them.

Like she knew that I would be there after she left. How could she know that?

No, it didn't make any sense. Neither my grandmother nor I had sensed a magical attack inside the mead hall. If she had been the one breaking the magical protections, we would've known.

And yet in my bones I knew it was true. At least, she had left that sign on purpose, for me to see. Maybe she didn't know what shape she had made or why, but she had made it on purpose. She had left it as a threat, to bring me running after her. I had understood it on some level the minute I saw it. That was why I had panicked.

But what if she had just a little magic? Not enough to draw our attention, but enough to sneak some poison into Dofri's mead. Was *that* possible?

I had no idea. I wished I could ask my grandmother.

I forced my legs to speed up my jog even as I pulled my phone out of my pocket. No missed calls. No texts. Had Neil managed to reach anyone at all?

I tried calling my grandmother, but her phone just rang and rang. She had never set up her voice mail. I couldn't text her while running, and I didn't dare stop.

So I called Andrew, but his phone went straight to voice mail. I waited for the beep and then said, "Andrew! I hope you're not answering because you're on your way back to Runde. I'm running to my grandmother's cabin now. I hope you'll be meeting me there soon. Bring Loke with you if you can."

Then I hung up and called Loke. His phone too went straight to voicemail. "Loke! I need your help. My grandmother may be in trouble. She went to meet Mandy Carlsen at her cabin in Runde. I think Mandy killed Dofri, and I think she's going to try to hurt my grandmother. Please, can you get there as fast as you can?"

I hung up, but almost immediately called him back to leave a second message. "Loke, I hope you're with Roarr. Bring him with you. Bring everyone you can."

By then, I was at the far side of the bridge at the top of the path that led down to my grandmother's cabin. This time I had to slow down because the steep path was too slippery to take at a run. It was frustrating, but every time I tried to speed up, I would feel my boot start sliding out from under me. If I cracked my skull open, I would definitely not get there in time.

At last I reached the road that ran from the lake shore to the meeting hall and turned to follow it to my grandmother's cabin.

But as soon as I could make its shape out through the snow-covered trees, I felt my heart clench.

Everywhere I looked, I saw the inverted thurs. It was in the snow, in the overlap of the tree branches, in the pattern of the wood walls of the cabin.

This was way too clear of a sign that I wasn't being paranoid. My grandmother really was in danger.

But if I just charged in through the front door, I would be in danger too. I needed to prepare for that.

I ran to the largest of the pine trees between the cabin and the road and hid behind it, out of sight of the cabin windows. I dropped my art bag onto the snow, the honey clanking loudly. It was a miracle the inside of my bag wasn't just one big sticky mess.

I sat down on the snow and grabbed my sketchbook, quickly turning to the first blank page. I didn't even take a moment to center myself first. I just started drawing.

I drew myself as a warrior, putting every kind of protection on my sketched self that I could think of. I was drawing so fast and so furiously that I wasn't even really seeing what I drew. I didn't stop until the end of my pencil snapped off and the wood tore a long scratch through the paper.

Only then did I see what I had drawn. I had drawn myself looking exactly like Thorbjorn. I was wearing his cloak and carrying his weapons. I was even standing the way he did when he expected a fight: a kind of eager leaning forward with my weight on the balls of my feet.

I touched the sketch, feeling how deeply my pencil had scoured the page.

It felt like Thorbjorn was there with me. I could almost smell his scent all around me. It made me feel so safe.

I shoved the book and pencil back into my bag and then stood up. I took one last look at my phone, but no one I had called had tried to contact me.

I put it away and pulled out my wand.

I was going to have to go in alone. But I was either as ready as I would ever be, or already too late.

I didn't want to even think about the second option there.

Wand raised, I headed towards the door.

# CHAPTER 19

*I* must have really been channeling something of Thorbjorn, because I didn't open the front door so much as kick it in. It smashed loudly against the wall.

Good thing I wasn't trying to be sneaky.

I quickly scanned the great room of the cabin, from the massive fireplace against the south wall to the kitchen tucked under the loft on the north side. There was no sign of my grandmother.

But there were two mugs sitting on the kitchen table. The chairs were pulled back as if someone had just gotten up and walked away. Only no one was there.

I waved my wand in front of my face. The entire cabin was filled with a whirling, chaotic energy. I could see it twisting in on itself in little eddies and vortexes. This wasn't magic I was looking at, but it wasn't exactly natural either. Had this been in the mead hall the night before and I had just missed seeing it? I didn't think so. It was too prominent, too hard to miss.

The whirling energy was chaotic, but there *was* a pattern. Something was generating all of it. I traced the patterns with my eyes until I found the source.

As if she knew she had been caught, Mandy stepped out of the shadows behind the corner of the fireplace.

"Hello, Ingrid," she said. "I was hoping I would see you."

"Where is my grandmother?" I demanded.

"Please," she said. "That doesn't matter."

"It does to me," I said.

"You'll see her soon enough," she said. Those words sounded like a threat, and yet her tone wasn't backing that up. She sounded... perky. Like an overly enthusiastic flight attendant.

"What's going on?" I asked, still brandishing my wand at her.

If she thought that was odd, she didn't show it. She just strolled across the great room to the kitchen and picked up one of the mugs to take a sip. She grimaced and brought both mugs to the sink to dump their contents down the drain.

"Fancy a cup of tea?" she asked. As if it were her kitchen we were both standing in.

"No," I said. But she took down two clean mugs, anyway. "I know you killed Dofri."

"Okay," she said, still too perky. "I figured you would when I saw you last night. You struck me as being very clever."

"You don't sound worried," I said.

She shrugged as she turned on the burner under the kettle that always stood ready on my grandmother's stove. "There's knowing and then there's proving. If you could prove anything, you would've brought the police with you."

"They're meeting me here," I said.

She laughed. "Really? So what you're doing here is just stalling for time? Keeping me distracted until the white hats arrive? Well, I heartily approve. Yes, this should be *fun.*" She opened the cupboard where my grandmother kept her tea and started sorting through the boxes, glancing at the labels but rejecting each.

"Is that the point of everything you've done? To have fun?" I asked.

"You've been talking to Neil," she said, pointing at me with a huge grin on her face.

"You know I have," I said.

"Yes, I do," she said. She settled on one of the boxes of tea and put a bag in each of the mugs.

"You don't actually think I'm going to drink that," I said. "I know you poisoned Dofri." Then a horrible thought struck me. "Where's my grandmother?" I demanded.

"She's fine," Mandy said, as if getting annoyed at repeating herself. "I swear I didn't poison her. Now sit down and let's talk."

"Talk about what?" I asked. I looked back over my shoulder, out the door that still stood open. But there was no sign of anyone coming. I glanced at my phone screen, but there was nothing there either.

Where was everybody?

"I assume you have questions," she said. The kettle started to whistle, and she held up a finger to silence me until she had poured water into each of the mugs. Then she brought them over to the table and sat down. "Come on. Sit. I'm not going to bite."

"I'm not drinking that," I said again.

She rolled her eyes at me. "Fine. Just sit, then. We're running out of time to talk. I'll answer your questions, but I want you to sit first."

She was patting the place next to her at the table, but I didn't take it. I sat down as far away from her as the little table would allow. And I kept my wand in my hand.

I wasn't sure exactly what good I could do with it, though. She had been the center of the chaotic energy, but there was nothing magical in her that I could see. She seemed to be just a normal person.

A normal person with a particular skill at generating chaos.

Still, attacking her with magic didn't feel like something I could feel comfortable doing.

"Why did you kill Dofri?" I asked.

"It wasn't exactly my plan A," she said with a laugh and took a sip of her tea.

"What was plan A?" I asked.

"Ugh," she said dramatically, pushing back her hair as if she were sweaty after some great effort. "Anything to get off my parents' property, you know? I couldn't get out of this town fast enough the first time. If I'm stuck here again now, at least I can get a little further away from the parental units. You know what I mean?"

"What does that have to do with Dofri?" I asked. "He was looking to buy a farm. And you'll pardon me for saying, you don't look like much of a farm girl."

"No, I'm not," she said. Then she grinned and pointed at me again. "You've definitely been talking to Neil. He said the same thing."

"So you're not trying to land a guy as a way of moving out of your parents' house?" I asked.

"First of all, I'm not in their house," she said. "Even I'm not that desperate. I'm just on their property, and it's only temporary. But it's not like there's much to pick from here in Runde."

"So leave," I said.

She laughed. "Sounds easy, right? Not so much. I'm stuck here. But I bet you're thinking I could always go back to my husband on the Iron Range."

"I thought he was your ex-husband," I said.

"Not quite yet. Sure, I'm seeing other people. And I know he hates it."

"How does he know?" I asked. She gave me a sly look. "What, you've been telling him?"

"I leave him voice mails," she said. A cat with a mouthful of mouse couldn't look so self-satisfied. "I've told him all about Dofri and all about Neil. Well, I had to embellish a little, didn't I? Neither one of them is exactly a catch. But I figure I'm only about three or four more phone calls away from him driving out here to fight for me."

"Is that what you want? Your husband back?" I asked.

"Eh?" she said with a shrug. "That's not really plan A either."

"Just out of curiosity, how many plans do you have?" I asked.

She laughed. "Oh, tons. We don't have time to go into all of them." She took another sip of tea, batting her eyes at me over the rim of her cup.

I didn't know what that look meant. I turned towards the open door again, but there was still no sign of anything approaching. Of course, the door faced the meeting hall at the end of the road. Andrew and the police would come from the other direction.

If he had even gotten my call.

"Sadly, plan A isn't really working out," Mandy said with a sigh.

"What's plan A?" I asked. "Or should I say 'who'?"

"You know me so well," she said. "No, really, that's quite astute of you. Plan A is Dave Wilson."

"Who's Dave Wilson?" I asked.

"The boy who had my heart all through high school," she said, putting her hand on her chest. Just in case I didn't know where her heart was. "Even when I married and moved away, I still always thought of Dave. He has my heart still. You know what that's like, don't you? I bet you do."

I ignored that question. "Where's Dave now?"

"Grand Marais," she said. "Not far away from here, but anything outside of Runde is an improvement. But seriously, he has a house on a bluff overlooking the lake. A gorgeous property, and the house is just perfect. It's like a castle, you know? The kitchen has a walk-in pantry, the master bedroom suite has not one but two bathrooms attached, and two walk-in closets as well. There's this grand staircase I can just see myself coming down when we're having parties, and all the vaulted ceilings are just divine. And there's a four-car garage. Four. Cars. Can you believe it?"

"It sounds like a lot," I said.

"It is," she said gleefully, not getting my point at all. "Dave has done very well for himself."

"Do you mean financially? Or the way it sounds like he success-fully evaded you?" I asked.

That perky glow was gone in a flash. Now she was glowering at me darkly. "I can have him any time I want him."

"Really? Then why make other plans? I mean, he's your plan A. And apparently a sure thing."

Just as suddenly as it had come, her anger passed. She shrugged as if she didn't have a care in the world and took another sip of tea. "I could have him. Make no mistake about that. But his wife is about to have their second child any day now, and he tells me they're so 'in love' and everything." She made the air quotes with her fingers and rolled her eyes. "So I'm letting him be for now. I mean, there are kids involved."

"And you're not that evil?" I guessed.

"I am definitely not looking to be anyone's step-mommy," she said and tossed her hair.

I watched that hair float through the air as if in slow motion. Now, even without my wand, I could see the eddies of chaotic energy she was stirring up. But I didn't think that was a good thing.

It was almost like I could see it clearly now because my normal vision was starting to go all black starbursts again.

"Something's wrong," I said, pressing a hand to my forehead.

"Definitely wrong," she agreed. "This should've started a quarter of an hour ago. You must have the constitution of a bear. Or at least of a man twice your size. But we got there in the end, didn't we?"

Poisoned. I was poisoned.

But I hadn't even touched that mug of tea.

I tried to get up from the table. I had a plan that involved running out of the cabin as fast and as far as I could.

But I couldn't get up from the chair.

"Poison," I said, my tongue so thick I could barely get the word out.

"Oh, no. Not you," she said with another laugh. That laugh echoed in my head like some sort of reverb effect on an experimental music album. "No, just a touch of sedation for you. Just like with grandma. You're going to take a little nap now. But I'll be there when you wake up."

I clutched my wand tightly in my hand, wishing it could give me strength somehow. I tried once more to push up from the chair. I made it halfway up, but it felt like the table lunged at me.

I was vaguely aware of feeling an impact as I collapsed across the table, then rolled to land on the floor.

I had dropped my wand, but it didn't matter. It was all I could do to hold on to the world. It was trying so hard to wash away from me.

162

I felt something vibrating against the back of my leg. My cellphone in my back pocket. Someone was calling me.

I tried to pull it out, but Mandy just leaned over me and snatched it out of my nerveless fingers. I peered up at her, but all I could see were the whirls of chaos all around her.

She wasn't generating it. But she sure knew how to take what chaotic energy there was in the world around all of us and whip it into a crazed frenzy. Did she even know she was doing that?

"There we go," she cooed to me as she crouched down beside me and gently closed my eyelids. I was powerless to resist. The darkness wanted me.

The last thing I heard was that irritatingly perky voice saying, "night-night!"

And then I was gone.

# CHAPTER 20

$\mathcal{I}$t felt like I was drowning in blackness for eons. Like my perception of it was a continuous timeline, and I could account for every second of it, one after another, in a seemingly endless succession.

So it was more than a little disorienting to open my eyes to find myself almost exactly where I had been when I had slipped away.

I was still in my grandmother's cabin.

I was no longer on the floor, but I was in the chair I had been sitting in before falling down.

Well, not so much sitting as slumping over the thick overlapping mass of rope that was holding me up against the chair back.

"There she is!" Mandy chirped. I lifted my head and focused on her, back in her chair again as well. But she was no longer drinking tea. No, she was sorting through my art bag, the one I had left hidden under the pine tree.

I tried to speak, but I didn't have control of my mouth yet. It felt like it was a lot of work just getting my two eyes to coordinate their movements.

"What's with all the honey?" Mandy teased as she set both of the jars side by side in the middle of the table. Then she peered back inside the bag and came out with my sketchbook.

"Are you an artist?" she asked, and started turning the pages. The folded-up sketch I had done by the bonfire fell out of where I had tucked it. She frowned at the image of Fasta, then unfolded the entire sheet. "Is this supposed to be me?" she asked, stabbing at the form of her standing by the table where Neil and Dofri sat. "No, that's not a good likeness at all. Look at my hair! It's all..." she waved her hand in a rolling motion as she searched for the word.

"Chaotic," I managed to say.

"Right. Chaotic. Does this look chaotic to you?" she pointed both her hands at her own hair. The peroxide she used to keep it blonde was clearly damaging her hair. I could tell from across the table that if I touched it, it would have the crunchy feel of dry straw.

But it was neatly arranged. She wasn't wrong about that.

Only I could still see the way she was churning up chaos all around her.

"Whatever," she said when I didn't answer. She turned her attention back to my bag. "Do you need this many pencils? It seems a bit excessive." She dug through the bottom of my bag, but when it didn't turn up anything she found interesting, she scrunched it up and pushed it away across the table.

"This is more interesting anyway," she said. The jars of honey were standing between us, so I didn't realize what she was referring to until she held up my bronze wand. "What were you doing with it before? Oh, yes." She waved it in front of her eyes with a theatrical look of concentration on her face.

My heart pounded hard. I had no idea what was about to happen. Could she use my wand? Deliberately or even accidentally? Could she break it?

But in the end she just tossed it on the table with a quick, "eh."

The wand rolled towards me, close enough to where I could reach out and grasp it.

If I weren't currently tied to the chair with knots so tight my hands were getting cold and numb.

"This is better, isn't it?" she said, and I looked up to see her once more holding up a wand. Only hers wasn't bronze. It was a wood so dark it was practically black, and polished so that it shone in the light. It looked not so much like obsidian as licorice.

"Blackthorn," she said. "I've had it since high school. The boy who was crushing on me made it for me as a gift. You'd think I'd remember his name, wouldn't you? He loved me like crazy, poor dear. It was never going to happen. Still, it's a cool gift, isn't it? Not that I carry it around with me all the time like you do, you freak. I had to go hunt it out of the boxes in the back of my car just now. But I wanted to show it to you. Nice, right?"

I could only summon the energy for a single word, so I had to make it count. "Dangerous," I said.

"Not to me," she said and spun it through her fingers. Then she set it on the table to pick up my phone. "I hope you will forgive me, but while you were napping, I've been texting with all your friends. They just needed to know that you were all right and there was no reason to panic. I think I've won them all over, but it was pretty tough there for a bit. You have very driven friends, you know?"

I wasn't ready to speak another word yet, but my eyes were quite capable of conveying my meaning.

"Oh, you think I overstepped? You know I had to. We still have to have that talk. Not the other one about, you know, *boys*. The real one. But I had to be sure first that we wouldn't be disturbed. Let's see." She opened my message app and started scrolling through. "Yes, Andrew was the hardest to convince. It was tough pretending to be you. You're always so cold to him in your texts! He clearly adores you. I don't know what you're thinking. But anyway, I got there in the end. He's agreed to go back to the hospital and wait for word from the medical examiner. I think he only did because the ME texted him that some results came in. Not that it matters. It won't prove anything."

I flexed my fingers, trying to keep the blood flowing. I couldn't move at all. Even my feet were tied to the legs of the chair. How had she managed it without help?

"Oh! I was going to ask you," she said as she continued scrolling through my texts. "What kind of crazy name is Loke, anyway? That's like that guy who's name I can't remember from high school. You know? The one who gave me the wand. The scrawny, pimply, almost albino pale kid who barely came up to my elbows. He had a weird name like that, too. Whatever! Loke was super easy to call off. You have him wrapped around your finger, I guess, right? So eager to please."

I tried shifting my shoulders to see if I could get any of the ropes to slip down, but they were too tight. I was pretty effectively trapped. But if she thought that meant I was helpless, I was going to prove to her how wrong she was.

"The last one was weird, though," she said, stopping on another text. "Your phone didn't recognize the number, and you didn't text them first. It just says, 'I was already on my way to you. Roar.' I mean, I'd put an exclamation point after that, wouldn't you? Roar! Does that mean anything to you?"

Clearly, Roarr hadn't noticed the autocorrect had changed his name. Was he on his way? Then what was keeping him?

"Wrong number," I said. There, I managed two whole words that time.

"You are such a liar," she laughed, then tossed my phone across the room. It landed on the couch with a soft thud. "Well, it's not like I don't know our time together is still limited. I swear I do. Are you ready for our real talk?"

"Why did you murder Dofri?" I asked.

She fisted her hands and shook them at the ceiling, all the while shrieking in inarticulate rage and frustration. "Look! He doesn't matter! It was just this impulse, you know? Maybe to get him away from Neil, maybe to get back at him for being *so rude* to me. Mostly to see if I could do it. I don't know. It doesn't matter!"

"What matters?" I asked.

"It matters that I know what you are," she said, and came over to sit on the edge of the table, her foot resting on the seat of my chair, pressing up against my knee. She put a hand on the back of the chair and leaned in close to my face. "I know what you and your grandmother are. And before you start interrupting, yes, your grandmother is still *just fine*. I didn't poison you, and I didn't poison her. And you'll be together real soon."

"Why not now?" I asked.

"Look, you'll be with her soon enough. In the meantime, you have to appreciate what I've figured out here. I mean, didn't you hear me? I know what you are."

"No, you don't," I said.

But she just leaned in closer until her lips were brushing against my ear as she said, "you're witches." She sat back and grinned at me. "I'm right, aren't I?"

I said nothing. My stomach plummeted like I was on the world's most intense rollercoaster, but I said nothing.

"You are. I've been watching since I came back into town. I mean, I always had my suspicions about Nora Torfa, even back in high school. But then last night you were there, and I just knew. You're here to take over as town witch, aren't you? Old Nora is starting to look a little faded, but you have such a fresh glow."

Could she really see that? But she had seen nothing when she had tried using my wand. She must be bluffing.

But I wasn't sure I believed she was.

"So that's my new plan A," she said and pushed herself away from the table to cross the great room. "I'm going to be the resident witch around here. Things are going to change in Runde, that's for sure! I am witchy-woman, here me roar!"

"I don't see any magic in you," I said. "Sorry."

"I can learn," she said with a dismissive wave. "I got around your spells already, didn't I? And I didn't even have to use my wand to do it. I just had to focus my attention for a moment. And boom! The poison was in Dofri's mead. That's when I knew. I could do it. I could do anything."

"You knew there was magic protecting the mead hall?" I asked.

"Yeah, that kid told me years ago. He warned me never to let Nora know I had that wand. I thought he was just being all goth or whatever, but I guess he was right, wasn't he?"

"That's all you did? Just put poison in Dofri's mead? There wasn't any spell or anything, it was just you doing it?"

"I focused, like I said." She screwed up her face as if demonstrating focus to me. "It was intense! Like I was struck by lightning. Well, you saw my hair, didn't you?" she said, gesturing towards the drawing still folded up on the table.

"So I tested myself, and I passed, and now I'm going to be the head witch or whatever. It's my destiny!"

"You don't need no man now? You have this plan instead?" I asked her.

"Are you kidding?" she laughed. "I'm going to have *all* the men. But first..." I looked over my shoulder to see her up on tiptoes, searching behind a stack of books on the fireplace mantel. She retrieved a small handbag and snapped it open.

When she turned back around, I saw the dull gleam of a gun in her hands.

"That's not very witchy," I said, hoping I didn't sound as terrified as I felt.

"Well, I can't be a witch with the two of you still around, can I?" she asked.

"How exactly do you think this all works?" I asked.

"I'll figure it out as I go. I'm clever!" she shouted at me. Then she aimed the gun at me and my heart just stopped.

"Don't," I said.

The patterns of chaos spinning around her were a blur of blinding speed. Standing in the middle of all that, how could she even hear herself think?

I almost started laughing hysterically. As if having coherent thoughts was a concern for Mandy Carlsen.

"Any last words?" she asked me, her voice a taunting purr.

And suddenly I felt like such an idiot.

My last word? It should've been my first word. I had been so consumed with trying to reach people with my phone that I had forgotten the one source of help that I could always call on.

Well, better late than never.

"Mjolner!" I shouted.

Mandy gave me a puzzled frown. Then I heard a soft meow coming from behind me as my cat walked in the open door.

To my surprise, Mandy reacted with absolute revulsion, moving quickly to put the table between her and Mjolner just as he leapt up to sit on my lap.

"Send him away! Send him away! I'm deathly allergic! Deathly!" she said. The gun was no longer aimed at me, as she used that arm to cover her mouth and nose.

I'd heard of people being allergic to cats, but *deathly* allergic? What was going on?

Mjolner climbed up the front of me to stand on my lap with his paws on my shoulder. He looked intently at something behind me, like he was waiting for something to happen.

Then I heard a loud bang, another door slamming open. I craned my neck to see almost directly behind me.

The door to my grandmother's bedroom stood wide open. And in that doorway stood my grandmother. She was still unwinding loop after loop of rope from around her body and letting it fall to the floor.

And the look in her eyes was pure murderous rage.

# CHAPTER 21

*I* was still trying to contort myself while tied to the chair, straining my neck to look at my grandmother, when the edge of the table caught me hard in the chest. Mjolner leapt clear just in time, but I had the wind knocked very painfully out of me.

The second blow toppled me over. I suppose the chair took most of it, but the back of my head hit the stone floor hard enough to make me see stars.

Then the gunfire started. I shook my head to clear it and looked up at my grandmother, but she wasn't Mandy's target.

No, her target was Mjolner. He howled his annoyance at her as he dodged from the cover of one piece of furniture to the next.

Mandy was sobbing hysterically as she fired. I didn't know why she was crying, but I was sure the tears in her eyes were messing with her aim. Which was a good thing.

I knew my cat could walk through walls, even though I had never seen him do it. I didn't want to test if that also worked with bullets.

"Put the gun down, child," my grandmother said, her voice the low rumble I knew meant she was adding a magical command to it. I tilted my head back again to look up at her. The head injury was making my vision blurry, but interestingly, this was more like the double exposure effect I sometimes got in the mead hall, where I could see two worlds at once.

I saw my grandmother dropping the remains of the rope that had bound her as she advanced towards Mandy and the gun. But I also saw her drawing in power from the magic within the walls of the cabin. Just like she had taken everything out of the mead hall.

I wasn't sure what sort of spell she was planning on using. But she might not even need to deploy it. Just the sight of her advancing so deliberately, unafraid, had distracted Mandy. More than distracted; she was just standing there with the gun only half-raised, gaping at my grandmother.

But the power in the walls was depleted before my grandmother's spell was quite strong enough. There wasn't enough there. Her cabin had only ever been hers, the only power within it what she had invested in it herself over the years. It wasn't an ancestral home with generations of power to draw from. And it definitely wasn't the mead hall.

I could see through both my overlapping views the moment when she gave up on pulling from the house and started drawing from herself. She was instantly paler, the shadows under her eyes darker, her gait shuffling and her back stooped.

"Mormor! I've got this!" I said. And I wished that it were true, but I was still tied to a chair. I wasn't capable of getting anything.

My grandmother almost had her spell woven together when she stumbled. She caught herself on the back of the couch and straightened back up at once, but that momentary lapse of concentration was enough for Mandy to break out of the gaping trance she had been in.

She raised the gun with a steady arm and took aim at my grandmother.

"Mandy, stop!" I commanded. I was lying flat on my back, still tied to a chair, my arms hopelessly numb, but I still had my voice. The voice I could magically amplify. I didn't have my grandmother's finesse. I tended to use too much magic. My voice would race right past being gently persuasive to being painfully loud, too much for anyone to tune out.

Which, in that moment, was exactly what I needed.

Mandy dropped the gun to cover her ears. I flinched as that gun hit the ground, but to my relief, it didn't go off.

"I've got her. Help Ingrid," my grandmother said as she swept past me, that spell still coalescing over her raised palm.

Wait, help Ingrid? Who was she talking to?

Before I could crane my head around to look towards her bedroom door, someone was hoisting my chair up off of the floor to rest once more on all four of its legs. Then I felt something sawing at the ropes, and they started to snap free one by one.

The sudden rush of blood was overwhelming, and I collapsed forward, trying to get my arms close to my stomach to warm them.

"All right, Ingrid?" Roarr asked as he leaned in to look into my eyes.

"How are you here?" I asked, but before he could answer, I heard that gun go off again.

Mandy must've pulled herself together and retrieved her weapon.

It was time to end this.

I looked around for my wand, but it was nowhere in sight. Both of the honey jars had tumbled off the tabletop along with the rest of the contents of my art bag, probably when Mandy had shoved the whole table into my chest. I had a very self-indulgent moment of sorrow as I watched that honey soak into the pages of my sketchbook. So much work, gone.

Then I saw the blackthorn wand. I lunged for it, dropping to my knees to sweep it up and pivot to aim at where I had seen Mandy last.

I didn't quite figure out where she had gone before the entire world started going crazy. A low rumble became an intense shaking as if we were in an earthquake.

This was followed by a sudden gale-force wind that blew through the open front door and across the cabin towards the windows over-looking the garden. They shattered all at once, the sound almost lost in the roaring of the wind. I think that Mandy might have shot them out when aiming for Mjolner, but the wind definitely finished the job.

But that glass didn't blow out into the garden as it should have.

The wind wasn't a straight-line force; it was more like a twister, and those shards were quickly caught up in it. They circled around the entire great room, cutting all of us in a thousand shallow cuts.

It was like having a tornado trapped indoors. A tornado full of glass.

Or so I thought. Then I looked outside the open door and saw a wall of dark gray cloud streaking past it. It was a wind filled with branches and gravel and bits of ice.

And it was lifting the cabin off of the ground.

I heard Mandy screaming into that wind, but it took her words before they could reach me. All I could make out was her rage. She was making her way towards me, step after step as she leaned into the changeable wind, but when she tried to raise that gun again, Roarr snatched it from her and tossed it out into the storm.

He was nearly sucked out after it, but caught himself on the door-frame just in time. He looked out, out and down, and his face turned a sickly shade of green. Then he pulled himself back inside, slamming the door shut behind him.

Then, for all the good it could possibly do in this situation, he locked it.

I had been out on a boat when the lake was in the throes of an epic storm, but the deck hadn't bucked anywhere near as wildly as the cabin floor was doing now. Worse, the stone floor was breaking apart piece by piece. I wasn't even sure how we had taken it up with us, but being caught in a supernatural twister, I guessed all bets were off.

Through the increasing numbers of holes in the floor, I could see the dark clouds rushing past, but occasionally there was a thinner layer of cloud and I could just make out the ground.

It was really far below us.

"Mormor!" I cried. "What spell is this?" I finally found her holding onto the rail at the bottom of the stairs with one hand. The other still held that spell she had been conjuring. It was a ball of light unbothered by the raging wind, but it was growing dimmer even as I looked at it.

"Not mine!" she shouted back. Then she ducked her head to one side, narrowly avoiding one of the kitchen knives. It hit the wall behind her and stuck there, but another soon joined it. And then another.

This wasn't the wind randomly throwing things around. Mandy had found the knife block. I could hear her cackling wildly.

At last my grandmother threw her spell. The ball of light grew brighter and larger the minute it left her grasp. By the time it reached the kitchen, it had a diameter the height of a person.

Plenty big enough to enclose Mandy. It glowed too brightly to look at for a few seconds, then settled to a more tolerable dark orange-yellow. Mandy was trapped inside like an insect caught in amber. I could see her trying to push her way out even as that ball started bouncing and flying around the room, mixing with the rest of my grandmother's worldly possessions.

"How do we get down?" Roarr shouted over the wind. Despite the green tinge that lingered in his complexion, he actually sounded really calm. Calmer than I felt.

"Ingrid has to stop," my grandmother said.

"Stop what?" I asked. She just pointed to my hand.

I had forgotten what I was holding onto. Mostly because I couldn't really feel it. My arms were still pretty numb from being tied so tightly.

But the coldness was gone. That was a good sign. The blood was back in my hands.

Only it was too warm, that wand in my hand. And as I looked down at it, that heat built to a searing intensity.

And I couldn't let it go.

"I can't drop it!" I said, shaking my hand like mad. It was like I had burnt marshmallow all over my fingers. I couldn't get it off, and it was cooking me.

"Ingrid," my grandmother said. She was suddenly there with me, her arms around me as if she needed me to anchor her. Which, since we were still flying and spinning through the air, was likely true. My feet felt glued to the ground as unbreakably as that wand was glued to my hand.

"I can't!" I said again.

"Just be calm," she said, running her hand down my arm until she was clasping my hand clasping the wand. "Deep breaths, Ingrid. We've practiced this."

I closed my eyes. Despite the chaos around us and the constant muffled screams of Mandy as she bounced from wall to wall within the safe confines of her amber ball, I managed to tune the whole world out.

The only thing I felt was the gentle warmth of my grandmother's soft hand on mine.

The only thing I heard was her voice.

"You can let it go now, Ingrid," she said. "Just open your fingers and let it fall. It's all right."

I nodded, then focused everything on unclenching my hand. Her fingers guided mine, gently helping pry them away one after another, until the wand fell to the floor with a deafening boom.

And then the house started to fall.

"Quickly!" my grandmother said, and I could see she was pulling more magic out of herself.

But she didn't have any left to give.

Then Mjolner was there beside me, looking up at me with a muffled meow.

My bronze wand was in his mouth.

I took it from him and again unleashed an absolutely overkill amount of power. I was panicking. I knew I needed to do something, but what I was doing was all wrong. It was like trying to stop a car to avoid an accident by slamming on the accelerator.

But my grandmother was there with me. Her magic wrapped over mine just as her hand had held mine before. The delicate strands of her spell caught and contained my blast of power.

Slowly, our plummet through the air became a gentle descent. By the time we reached the ground, it was barely a jostling. Like a boat, bumping up against a dock after a calm day out on the lake.

Roarr unlocked the door and threw it open. Then he started to laugh.

My grandmother joined him in the doorway to see what was so funny.

Despite everything that had happened, we had brought the house back down exactly where it was meant to be. The pine tree in the front yard was looking a little damaged by the wind, having lost a number of thick branches, but it still stood tall and proud.

And between us and the tree were Andrew and the officer from the sheriff's department, Foster.

"What did I just see here?" Foster asked, taking his shades off to rub at his eyes.

"We get strange weather here sometimes. Being so close to the lake and yet in a sort of valley. You know?" Andrew said. He was trying to smile and bit his lip at the same time, uncertain if Foster was going to buy it.

"Strange weather? I would swear I just saw this cabin fall out of the sky like something out of *The Wizard of Oz*," Foster said.

"No, it was here the whole time," Andrew said. "Although that wind did a number on it. I guess it was a mini-gale or something." He shot my grandmother and me a desperate look. He knew he wasn't remotely convincing.

Then my grandmother made the smallest of gestures, unseen by anyone but me.

And Foster blinked, then put his shades back on. "Well, I'll have to take your word for the strangeness of the weather, not being a local myself. Now, Mrs. Torfa, I understand you have a guest in your house? Mandy Carlsen?"

"What do you need with Mandy?" I asked, but only to distract his attention long enough for my grandmother to undo the amber bubble spell and let Mandy go.

"She's under arrest," he said.

"For Dofri's murder?" I asked. Andrew flinched, and I remembered too late that Dofri was a John Doe in Foster's world. Oops.

But he didn't seem particularly thrown by the question. He just stepped closer to the door, a hand resting on the gun in his belt.

"I don't know that name," he said. "But she is wanted for two murders and a third attempted murder. Is she here?"

"I am!" Mandy said, pushing past my grandmother, Roarr and me to get out into the yard. I thought she was going to try to flee arrest and started to raise my wand to stop her.

But she just threw herself into a startled Foster's arms. "Please, get me out of here! These witches are crazy!"

# CHAPTER 22

$\mathcal{I}$t was strange to step outside of a house that had just been wrecked by a tornado and realize that outside, it was still February.

Foster and another officer who had been waiting by the car took Mandy away as soon as they were done reading her her Miranda rights. I wasn't sorry to see her go.

But I was sorry to see the remains of my grandmother's cabin. From the inside, it had seemed like we would just need to spend a day or two cleaning up and replacing all the windows. But from the outside it was clear from the way it was listing heavily to one side, the roof sagging so low it was nearly ready to split in two, that repairs were out of the question. It would have to be demolished.

"Mormor?" I said. She, too, was looking at the remains of her home with deep sadness.

"I built this place myself," she said, her voice low but inflectionless. "When your mother wanted to go to high school out here in this world, I built this place for the two of us to live. I've been here ever since. I've slept here every night until last night."

"We'll figure something out," I promised her.

She nodded, but I knew she wasn't really hearing me. If she were, she would've objected. I knew how she felt about my house in Vill-mark. She had grown up there, but she didn't feel at home there.

"I'm guessing you won't need help finding a place to stay?" Andrew said as he approached us with blankets in his arms. He must've gotten them from the police car before it had departed. He handed one to me and draped the other around my grandmother's shoulders himself.

I was still wearing my parka and hat. I had taken off my mittens before I had charged into the house to rescue my grandmother, but they were still in my pockets.

But I wrapped the blanket around myself, anyway. Even though I didn't think it was cold making me shake.

"If you do, I know I can find any number of volunteers with a spare room for you," Andrew went on.

My grandmother finally snapped out of her reverie. "No, we're fine. But thank you, Andrew."

"You don't have to come to Villmark if you'd rather not," I said. "I'm sure Tuukka would have you."

"No, we have to go back to Villmark," she said.

But saying Tuukka's name had set off a cascade of thoughts in my own head, and I found myself lunging at Andrew to clutch at his sleeve. He looked at me with alarm.

"Neil! Is he okay?" I asked.

"He's fine," Andrew said, giving me a puzzled look.

"Are you sure? Foster said there had been multiple murders," I said.

"Right, I'm guessing you missed some texts," Andrew said.

"At this point, I'm not even sure where my phone is," I said, looking towards the house.

"Don't try to go back in there," he said, his tone firm. "It's clearly not safe. After the... what, wind storm? Cyclone? I mean, what was that?"

"I'll explain that later," I said. "First, the murders?"

"Right," Andrew said. "Well, I guess I missed seeing texts from you first. I'm sorry about that. I was still at the hospital waiting to hear what the poison was determined to be. Foster was there checking in as well, and we were chatting when he got a call from the sheriff's office. Mindy Carlsen's husband had just been found dead in Saint Louis County."

"She was a police suspect?" I asked, a little ashamed they had been one step ahead of me. Not that connecting those sorts of dots wasn't their job more than mine.

"Not until they found her husband. He was poisoned. The initial exams of both victims made it seem likely the same substance was used on both the husband and on Dofri," Andrew said. "That's how she became a suspect."

"But she told me she was still talking with him," I said. "No, wait. Leaving him voice mails. But she said she was trying to make him jealous enough to drive out here and fight to get her back."

"He had been dead for weeks when his brother finally broke into the house and found him," Andrew said. "The police don't have a time-line yet, but it certainly sounds like she killed him before she came here. For all we know, they weren't even planning to get divorced before she killed him."

"But why? It makes no sense," I said.

"Clearly, she was crazy," Andrew said. Looking past him, I could see my grandmother giving me a significant look, but I couldn't tell exactly what she was trying to communicate to me.

"So two murders," I said.

"And an attempted murder," Andrew said. "A man from Grand Marais was flown to the Twin Cities for specialized care. He's in bad shape. They're not sure if he's going to pull through."

"Dave Wilson," I said.

Andrew's eyebrows shot up in surprise. "Yes. You know him?"

"No, Mandy mentioned him. He was the man she actually wanted, apparently. An old flame," I said. I felt sick to my stomach.

"Well, so much as there's good news here, it wasn't the same sort of poison that killed Lisa. It was cyanide in all three of these cases. Mandy made it herself from cherry pits. I'm not sure why she used that; she also had ricin in her car, which is far deadlier."

"I don't think she was approaching things in an entirely rational way," I said. "She really seemed to think her husband was still alive back home, for one."

"She'll get a full psychological evaluation, I'm sure," he said. "It's going to be a tough time for her family, I'm afraid. I went with Foster to her parents' house first. They didn't even know she was back in town. She lied about that. Apparently, she was living out of her car. She parked it a bit further down the road from here, and Foster and I stopped there first. Until we saw the tornado."

"She mentioned having her stuff in boxes in her trunk," I said, not mentioning the wand.

"Yes, we searched it. A lot of guns. A couple of pipe bombs, even. I guess she was looking to expand beyond poisoning potential romantic partners soon. It's a good thing you stopped her in time," Andrew said.

"But why? I don't get it at all," I said.

"What's to get? She was nuts," Andrew said. "Lucky for you she is, too. Foster isn't going to pay any mind at all to what she said about the two of you being witches."

"And how did she figure that out, I wonder?" I said.

"I'm sure we'll know more after she's questioned at the station," Andrew said. "I'm going to go up the hill a bit to where the cell reception is better. I want to tell Foster about the connection between Mandy and Dave Wilson."

I had the feeling that Foster had already heard all about it directly from Mandy, but I just nodded and let him go. My grandmother had not stopped sending me looks that I was beginning to understand meant she wanted to talk to me. I watched Andrew climb the hill, then turned to my grandmother.

"I'm sorry I didn't get here sooner," Roarr said, making me jump when he suddenly appeared at my elbow. I thought he had already made himself scarce.

"I'm just happy you were here at all," I said. "It seems like you're the one who untied mormor."

"Yes, he crept in through the bedroom window and cut me loose," my grandmother said.

"Your text said you were already on the way?" I said to him.

For some reason, it seemed like that question embarrassed him. He flushed redly and looked down at his feet. "I guess you figured out I was running my own investigation into things."

"That had become apparent," I said.

"I had just spoken with one of Mandy's old high school friends before I came here. She had some pretty scary things to say about Mandy. She had heard about Dave Wilson falling ill and was certain Mandy was behind it. I left there at once to come here and find you. I wanted to compare notes and help you figure out what to do next. But I was too late."

"You were right on time," my grandmother said.

"Yes, you really were. Thanks," I said. "But why were you investigating this at all? None of it affected you or anyone you know, did it?"

"No more than it did you," he said, raising his chin. "I only intended to be helpful."

"You could've just asked to help out," I said.

"And you would've sidelined me," he said. "You always do. You still don't trust me."

I opened my mouth, but then had to close it again. I knew he was right. I tended to rely on my closer friends for help, despite the fact that Roarr always seemed to be there, trying to make a contribution. Nilda and Kara had heavy responsibilities now, and Loke was often just not there. I really should be turning to Roarr more often for help.

"I won't sideline you again," I promised him.

He nodded, but he didn't look convinced.

"My goodness, you ladies know how to party," Loke said as he strolled into the yard. "And here it is only mid afternoon. That must've been one heck of a high tea."

"Didn't you get any of my texts?" I asked.

"I'm not totally sure I know where my phone is," he admitted, not looking the least apologetic.

"Then why are you here now?" I demanded.

"Well, I'm afraid it's not good news," he said. "The council sent me."

"The council sent you," I repeated skeptically.

"I know. We can all just die of shock now," he said without a trace of humor. "Seriously, they know that Mandy was arrested for the murder. They assume that is the result of your investigation. Which means your investigation is done. It's time to go back to Villmark."

"But I still have questions," I objected.

"I think the council is correct," my grandmother said. Those were very nearly the last words I ever expected to hear her say.

"What? How?" I gasped.

"We know Mandy killed Dofri. They found her collection of poisons and will soon know which one was used. But none of that is a Villmark matter."

"But I still don't understand *why*," I said. "I don't find chalking it all up to crazy remotely adequate."

"Don't you? Neither do I," my grandmother said. But then she turned to Loke. "I need to ask a boon of you. A rather large one. I think you're the only one who can do this."

"Color me intrigued," Loke said. "What is it?"

"Within my cabin is a blackthorn wand. Ingrid touching it is what caused this tempest to tear my house apart. Not that I'm blaming you, dear," she added to me.

"What's going to happen when I touch it?" Loke asked. But he didn't sound frightened of her possible answer. In fact, his eyes were bright with excitement.

"Why don't you go find out?" my grandmother said to him. "Ingrid and I better hurry to the council hall. But once you've disposed of it, come find me and tell me how it went."

"Dispose of it where?" he asked.

"I believe you know a few suitable bogs," she said.

"You can't put it somewhere anyone is going to find it," I objected.

"Believe me, no one is going to find the bog I'm thinking of," Loke said with a wink. And then he disappeared into the ruined remains of the cabin.

"Was that wise?" I asked my grandmother. "Shouldn't we... I don't know, study it?"

"It was the wisest of the choices before me," she said with a sigh. "It isn't safe for either of us to handle, but especially you. Loke is the best choice. I'm sure he'll be fine. But now we have to go."

"But Andrew hasn't come back yet," I said. I could see him still halfway up the path to the highway, his phone pressed to his ear. He was facing the other way. Even if I waved to him, he wouldn't see me.

"I'll wait here and explain for you," Roarr said.

"But I don't know when we'll have the mead hall open again. Unless you have a plan for that?" I asked my grandmother hopefully.

But the smile she gave me was a sad one. "Everything will work out in the end, I'm sure. But the road to get there may be longer than you'd like."

"What does that mean?" I asked. My hands were in fists and I wanted to bellow up to the skies.

Just like Mandy had done.

What was wrong with me?

"I do hope Loke hurries with that wand," my grandmother said as she looped her arm through mine and led me away from the cabin.

"Why?" I asked, more irritably than I had intended.

"Clearly bonding with that wand is effecting you," she said. "But don't worry. Once Loke has gotten rid of it, you'll go back to your old self again."

"It bonded with me? That's why it stuck to my hand like that?" I asked.

"It's been trying to bond with Mandy for who knows how many years," she said.

"Since high school," I said, remembering what Mandy had said.

"But she has no power herself. It did everything it could to work through her, but the damage it could do was limited."

"She had guns and pipe bombs ready to go," I said.

"Yes. It *is* a good thing we stopped her," she said.

"You talk about this wand like it was sentient," I said.

"No, it had no mind as we know it. It just had an impulse for chaos," she said. "And before you ask, no, I have no idea what came first. Perhaps Mandy was already mentally disturbed, and the wand took advantage of that. Or perhaps the wand's influence deranged her mind. I think it was a bit of both. They fed off each other. I hope when Loke destroys the wand and releases its influence over you that it also helps poor Mandy. But I fear it's been too long. The damage has been done. And she can't undo any of the things she did over the last few days."

"But she's had it since high school. It showing up now isn't related to the other artifacts turning up. Is it?" I asked.

"That's the real question, isn't it?" my grandmother sighed.

Then we walked in silence the rest of the way up to Villmark.

# CHAPTER 23

*A*s much as Loke had said we were to report right away to the council, my grandmother still had us stop at my house in Villmark first. We cleaned up and got dressed in the more traditional garb that was considered more council-appropriate.

I didn't think it was going to help our case much, but it couldn't hurt. And since Brigida apparently knew all, like the very instant someone in Runde was placed under arrest, she knew we were back inside the town limits.

And that I hadn't even said goodbye to my friends. I hoped she knew that, too. I was burning with anger over that. Which I was pretty sure meant that Loke hadn't destroyed that wand yet. It was weird, being that angry, but at the same time feeling like it wasn't *my* anger.

I didn't like the feeling much at all.

The sun was low over the western hills when we finally pushed open the heavy doors and walked into the council hall. It was, as always, severely underlit. Even though it was approaching dusk outside, I still had to let my eyes adjust to the gloom within before guiding my grandmother close to the dais.

No one was there, but someone had left a stool before the dais. I helped my grandmother sit down on it but remained standing myself.

She wasn't retreating to that catatonic state from the day before, but she was still not right. The short walk from my house had left her winded, and walking with her arm through mine, she had just felt so frail.

My grandmother was the farthest thing from frail.

"It was a big day," she said to me, as if reading my mind. "But it's over. We can rest now."

My emotions had been charging away with me again. I took a deep breath and forced myself to calm down.

Then, quite suddenly, my mind suddenly felt clear and calm. As proficient as I was with breathing techniques, I knew this was nothing I had done.

My grandmother smiled but said nothing.

"It's going to take more than a day for you to recover. Isn't it?" I asked her.

"So much more," she said.

We waited in silence as the minutes ticked by. I had no idea what the council was up to. Perhaps arguing the best course of action amongst themselves. But at least I was only mildly annoyed at being left standing around. The anger was gone.

Then the doors behind us opened again and Roarr and Loke came in together. Loke met my grandmother's gaze and gave her a little nod, then gave me a thumbs up.

"We're here if you need us," he mouthed at me. Then he and Roarr stood to the side of the hall, half in the shadows, and looked towards the dais.

Finally, there was the bang of another, unseen door opening and the three members of the council came out to take their seats on the dais. Haraldr caught my eye, and I could see he was pleased about something.

I wasn't feeling too pleased with myself. I had been meant to be forging a working relationship with the rune of chaos, and instead, I had become an instrument of chaos itself. That couldn't be a good thing.

"The woman Mandy Carlsen is the murderer of Dofri. Is that your conclusion?" Brigida asked without preamble the minute she sat down.

"Yes. We believe it was partly a crime of passion," I said. "Not related to the property matter or even the honey. It had nothing to do with Dofri being from Villmark."

"Partly a crime of passion, and partly what?" Valki asked.

"Well," I said, exchanging a nervous glance with my grandmother. "From what Mandy said, she knew there was magic protecting the mead hall. She said she did it just to see if she could succeed. But she wasn't using magic. We would've felt that if she had. She was just a force of chaos, totally natural if exceedingly strong."

"But was so much magic necessary in apprehending this individual?" she asked.

"We saw the cabin flying up into the sky from the meadow," Valki said. There was a little twinkle to his eye, as if he were sorry he had missed being inside the cabin when all the fun was happening.

"That wasn't our magic," I said.

"Whose magic was it, then?" Brigida asked.

"There was a blackthorn wand that was drawing down chaos," my grandmother said. "It's been dealt with."

"The poison used was not from Villmark, and neither was the murderer. The Runde world is already taking over the matter. There is nothing more to be done. Justice has been served," I said.

"Perhaps," Brigida said. "But just because you've cleared Nora Torfudottir of the charge of murder by poisoning doesn't remove her from all blame. There is still the matter of the protections she has sworn to maintain. Why did they fail?"

"I-" my grandmother started to say, but Brigida cut her off.

"I am interested in what Ingrid Torfudottir has to say in this regard," she said. "Please, let your granddaughter speak first. Let her give us her assessment."

I felt myself bristling with anger on my grandmother's behalf, but she just gave my hand an encouraging squeeze then tipped her head towards the council, inviting me to speak to them.

"I think it was a mistake, separating me from my grandmother," I said. "She had shifted some of the work maintaining those spells to me. Shifting it back, it was too much for her. She can't do it alone any longer."

"Then you are finally seeing the sense in what we've told you," Brigida said. "The mead hall must be closed."

"No," I said.

But, "only for a time," my grandmother said.

"Mormor," I said, shocked.

"Only for a time, Ingrid," she said.

"Then it is agreed," Brigida said, slapping her ringed hands on her knees like a judge striking a gavel. I so badly wanted to object, but my grandmother's hand squeezed mine again, begging me to stay silent. Brigida went on, "there is the further matter of whether it is time for the old volva to step down and the new to step up."

She had more to say, but I couldn't bear to let her say it. I put my hands on my hips and summoned all my warrior energy as I said firmly, "no."

"No?" Brigida asked.

"No," I said again. "That time is not now. It's not even soon. Look, if you're so aware of what happened down in Runde, it should be completely obvious to you what I mean."

"Explain," Brigida said, sitting back in her chair as if indulging me by listening.

"I nearly lost control of everything," I said.

"That was the wand, though, correct?" Valki said.

"It doesn't matter why I was out of control," I said. "The point is, I had power but no control. That is always my problem. And it will continue to be a problem for some time yet. That's part of what I'm learning. Haraldr is teaching me rune craft, and I appreciate that. But on my own, I'm also working on mastering control of magic itself. I'm not there yet. I'm not even close. And I won't get there without a lot more practice."

Brigida said nothing. Her face was too impassive for me to even guess what she was thinking.

"My grandmother's power is waning. I guess there's no denying that now," I said miserably. "I've been denying it for some time, but it's true. But her waning power is still a great power. It could be decades before it wanes down to a point where it's too little to be of any use. But her control?" I broke off with a rush of expelled air, then pressed my fingers to the bridge of my nose. "It's difficult to explain."

"Try," Brigida said.

"It's like when I use magic, I'm using a paint sprayer on the widest setting. But mormor, she has the finest of brushes. And the difference matters," I said.

Okay, bad analogy. I had no idea if Brigida even knew what a paint sprayer was, let alone how one worked. I was really messing this up.

"If I may," Haraldr said. I didn't know if he was asking me, but I nodded for him to continue, just in case.

"Go on," Brigida said with a sigh.

"What Ingrid is trying to explain to you is that she and her grandmother need to work together for the time being," he said. "Neither of them alone is volva for us now. But the two of them together can fulfill that role."

"Better than one alone," my grandmother said.

Brigida sat forward in her chair and traded a long look with Valki. Then she sat back again. "Very well," she said. "Then it's settled."

"Wait, what's settled?" I asked.

"That you will share the role for the foreseeable future," she said.

"But does that mean she has to stay in Villmark?" I asked.

"Obviously," she said.

"No, not in Villmark," my grandmother said.

Brigida narrowed her eyes at my grandmother. "Not in Runde."

"No, of course not," my grandmother said. "I know better than any of you how run down I am. I know I need a long recovery, and that can't be rushed. But it would be better if I could make that recovery elsewhere."

"Where?" Valki asked.

"Deeper within the heart of my ancestress Torfa's original spells," she said.

"What's that mean?" I asked, afraid we were about to spend the next weeks or even months living in the cave by the bonfire.

"Closer to Old Norway," she said to me. Then she looked to Brigida. "May I trouble you for a bowl of water?"

"Certainly," Brigida said, and waved a hand in the air. In a moment Haraldr's assistant Fulla was there, a bowl full of water in her hands. She set it on the floor at my grandmother's feet.

"Help me down," my grandmother said to me. I held her hands as she got up from the stool and settled herself on the stone floor before that basin of water.

Then she reached into the neckline of her dress and pulled out a simple ring hanging from a leather cord. She untied the cord and dropped the ring into the bowl of water.

"Can you do this?" I asked her in a whisper. She had nothing left in her. I knew she didn't.

"The ring does it," she whispered back to me. Then she blew over the surface of the water until it was a kaleidoscope of ripples. "Frór," she called.

The ripples died away, but when the water was still, it wasn't my grandmother's reflection I saw in the water. It was Frór's.

"Nora," he said, as if she had just called him up on her phone. What was he doing on his end? Looking into a pond? Staring into space? He certainly seemed to be making eye contact with my grandmother.

"Frór, I would like to stay at your house, if I may impose on you," she said.

"The old place?" he asked.

"Yes, in the north, by the lake shore," she said. "I need to rest there for a time."

"Ah, Nora. You know I've always considered that place as much yours as mine. No permission needed. Imposition indeed," he grumbled.

"I'll be bringing Ingrid with me," she said.

"As if I'd object to that," he said, still sounding surly. But then something passed over his face. "You really need this, don't you?"

"I'm afraid I do, yes," she admitted.

"More than you did the other day when I begged you to go there?"

"Now, Frór. Don't start picking fights with me," she said.

"Wouldn't dream of it," he said.

Then he was gone.

"Ingrid can't go with you," Brigida said. "She's needed here."

"What part of both of us or neither of us didn't you understand?" I asked. She shot me a dark look, but I refused to back down.

"They won't be so far away they can't be called in if needed," Haraldr said mildly. "And I've been meaning to take longer walks myself. It will be no burden to me to travel there to continue my lessons with Ingrid."

"Then it's settled," Valki said, clapping his hands together.

Brigida looked like she was about to jump to her feet and take the argument up a notch. But in the end, she just nodded.

Then the council filed out of the room again. My grandmother retrieved her ring from the water and tied it back around her neck before taking my hands. I pulled her to her feet, and we walked outside to where the light was better.

Loke and Roarr came out with us. "You're going to need supplies," Loke said. "Roarr and I will be happy to be your delivery people."

"The wand?" my grandmother asked him.

"I know it's gone," I told her. "I felt it let me go."

"It's at the bottom of the deepest bog I know," he said. "It sank like a stone. I didn't even have to weight it down. I also think it was trying to talk to me."

"Really? What did it say?" she asked.

"Oh, you know. Things," he said with a grin.

"I won't be at all surprised if you end up coming to a sticky end," she said, narrowing her eyes at him. But then she relented and clapped him on the shoulder. "But now I owe you a boon. That's no small thing."

"No, it's not," he agreed.

"Use it wisely," she said. "If that's at all possible for you."

"Where are we going, exactly?" I asked. It was now fully dark and getting too chilly for traditional Villmark clothes. I longed for my parka.

"Frór's cabin. You were there as a child, if you remember," she said.

I ran through my memories. When he had spoken of his northern cabin to me before, I had assumed it, too, was in the woods. But now that I knew better, I remembered an endless expanse of grayish-blue lake all around a stony prominence. Only a single, treacherous path led up to the lonely cabin.

"And that's a good place to recover your magic?" I asked. It felt to me mainly a good place to slip and die in a hurry. How had I been allowed to run free there as a child?

"The best," she assured me. "You and I working together, we'll be ready in no time."

"Ready for what?" Roarr asked.

"Ready to restore the mead hall," she said. "I trust I'm not the only one who needs that mead hall in their lives?"

"I met Lisa there. It's where my heart still lives," he said. Those words should've sounded silly, too poetic. But it was clear that he meant them, and I found myself blinking back tears on his behalf.

"We all need it. Even the ones who think they don't," Loke said, casting a side eye towards another band of armed Villmarkers returning from patrol to relax at one of the other mead halls.

My grandmother pulled Roarr close to her side and started dictating a shopping list to him. I could see him nodding, trying to keep up, before giving up and digging a little notebook out of his pocket. He flipped past pages I was just sure contained his notes into the investigation of Dofri's murder before finding a blank one to scribble my grandmother's list on.

"He would've solved this faster than me if magic hadn't been a factor," I said to Loke.

"You think so?" he said. "But magic *was* a factor. So."

We walked on in silence for a moment, then I said, "the wand really spoke to you?"

"Didn't it speak to you?"

"I don't think so," I said. "I think it just plowed right through me. I didn't like it."

"Really? I found it rather... seductive. I was tempted to keep it, actually."

"You were? But in the end you threw it away like my grandmother told you to?"

"You don't think I did?" he asked me with a grin. "Rest your mind. It had a hold on you, but that hold is gone now. You're safe. But if you hadn't touched it first? I totally would've kept it."

"I need to figure out where it came from," I said.

"Well, you won't be able to do that where you're going," he said.

"Oh, you know all about where we're going?"

"Oh, yes," he said. "I wander a lot, you know. I know that part of the world very well."

"And?" I prompted.

"And I can promise you just one thing. You'll experience things there that you've never experienced before."

"Well, that's just great," I grumbled.

Ever since coming to Runde, experiencing things I'd never experienced before was kind of a daily thing. I could tell Loke meant something more, something bigger. But I had no idea what that could be.

But I knew I was about to find out.

# CHECK OUT BOOK SEVEN!

The Viking Witch will return in Slaying on the Lake Shore, out February 15, 2022 and available for preorder now!

Spring, the season of renewal, finally arrives on the North Shore of Lake Superior, and Ingrid Torfa finds herself in a strange new situation.

On vacation.

She and her grandmother spend their days resting and recuperating in an old cabin overlooking the shores of Lake Superior. She can see modern ships pass by along the shipping lanes on the horizon. But everything around her? Strictly from the Viking Age. Not even the lost Norse village of Villmark lies so far in the past as this lonely cabin.

But her restful vacation comes to a sudden end when a stranger knocks on their door. His presence disrupts their quiet lakeside lives even before he turns up dead.

Now Ingrid must figure out who wanted the strange old man dead. Because the next target just might be her.

Slaying on the Lake Shore, Book 7 in the Viking Witch Mystery Series!

# THE WITCHES THREE COZY
# MYSTERIES

In case you missed it, check out Charm School, the first book in the complete Witches Three Cozy Mystery Series!

Amanda Clarke thinks of herself as perfectly ordinary in every way. Just a small-town girl who serves breakfast all day in a little diner nestled next to the highway, nothing but dairy farms for miles around. She fits in there.

But then an old woman she never met dies, and Amanda was named in her will. Now Amanda packs a bag and heads to the big city, to Miss Zenobia Weekes' Charm School for Exceptional Young Ladies. And it's not in just any neighborhood. No, she finds herself on Summit Avenue in St. Paul, a street lined with gorgeous old houses, the former homes of lumber barons, railroad millionaires, even the writer F. Scott Fitzgerald. Why, Amanda can practically hear the jazz music still playing across the decades.

Scratch that. The music really, literally, still plays in the backyard of the charm school. Because the house stretches across time itself. Without a witch to protect this tear in the fabric of the world, anything can spill over. Like music.

Or like murder.

Charm School, the first book in the complete Witches Three Cozy Mystery Series!

# ALSO FROM RATATOSKR PRESS

The Ritchie and Fitz Sci-Fi Murder Mysteries starts with Murder on the Intergalactic Railway.

For Murdina Ritchie, acceptance at the Oymyakon Foreign Service Academy means one last chance at her dream of becoming a diplomat for the Union of Free Worlds. For Shackleton Fitz IV, it represents his last chance not to fail out of military service entirely.

Strange that fate should throw them together now, among the last group of students admitted after the start of the semester. They had once shared the strongest of friendships. But that all ended a long time ago.

But when an insufferable but politically important woman turns up murdered, the two agree to put their differences aside and work together to solve the case.

Because the murderer might strike again. But more importantly, solving a murder would just have to impress the dour colonel who clearly thinks neither of them belong at his academy.

Murder on the Intergalactic Railway, the first book in the Ritchie and Fitz Sci-Fi Murder Mysteries, available digitally on Amazon and in print everywhere books are sold.